The Meantime

Bernie MacKinnon

Houghton Mifflin Company
Boston

Library of Congress Cataloging in Publication Data

MacKinnon, Bernie.
  The meantime.

  Summary: A black family finds life in a middle class
suburb full of trials and tribulations as they try to
cope with the hostility of their neighbors and schoolmates.
  [1. Afro-Americans—Fiction.   2. Prejudices—Fiction]
I. Title.
PZ7.M1997Me   1984   [Fic]   84-12896
ISBN 0-395-35387-4
PA ISBN 0-395-61622-0

Printed in the United States of America

AGM 10 9 8 7 6 5 4 3 2 1

The Meantime

For my brothers and sisters

In the meantime, which is
the time in which we all live,
good night.

—Bill Moyers,
signing off

September 27th

I am looking at the rock. I'm at the kitchen table and the rock is in front of me; I haven't touched it since putting it there. Again I glance at the window. Jagged glass teeth rim the hole, cracks radiating like spider legs. Across the street, a white neighbor—don't know his name—is mowing his lawn. I see him glance over a couple of times, almost imperceptibly. It's Sunday.

I look back at the rock. Slowly, before my stare, it becomes something new. It seems to be alive, staring back with a hundred mica eyes: "You can throw me away, but I'll be back—yeah, I'll be back." More than just a symbol of this moment, this morning, it seems a fist-sized generator of the numbness I feel. Strange—strange, like the fact that I'm still gripping the broom across my lap. I swept up the glass an hour ago.

My sister, Rhonda, walks in and glances down at me. Her face is hard, somber, but at least that's some kind of expression, indicating that as far as she's concerned, she has grasped this thing for all it is. Rhonda's a year younger than I, a junior at school. A beautiful girl, getting more so every day, it seems. Long limbs and a

3

smooth, queenly face; poised and bright too. But she has this way of looking at me sometimes, as if trying to choke from me one of her own flat declarations. I don't speak. She leans against the counter, picks up a magazine and starts flipping through it without looking at the window.

"Oppression"—that's a central term of Rhonda's, a real favorite. "Injustice" is another. For some reason those aren't words I'd be inclined to use, and even less so now. Isn't that an irony? "Irony" is a favorite word of my English teacher.

From the front door my mother's voice sounds clearer now, but less steady. The white cop sounds genuinely sympathetic, and Mom is allowing herself some expression.

"It's just a real shock, you know. We've been here almost two months and we've had no real trouble. It seemed like a nice neighborhood."

"I know, ma'am. It's a damn shame."

"Then this, all of a sudden. I just don't know what to expect next."

"Well, it could be just a random act. Not connected with any of this other trouble."

She sighs.

I was reading my history in the living room when the window broke. I remember not breathing for a moment: "Please let it be a baseball," I thought. "Some kid's baseball." But as I ran to the kitchen I heard the car screech away, and I knew.

"Try not to worry too much," the cop is saying.

"I'll try."

"My partner's checking the neighbors for some description of the car."

4

"I sure wish we'd seen it."

"We'll be checking back with you."

"Thank you, thanks very much."

"You're welcome, Mrs. Parrish."

Across the street, another cop is talking to the lawn-mower guy, who's shaking his head.

My mother comes in and stops to look at the window. While doing dishes she has often smiled and said what a nice view it is out there. Now her eyes look blurred, as mine probably do.

Rhonda drops the magazine and crosses her arms. "Daddy's not up yet. He's gonna be . . ."

"Let him sleep," Mom sighs, waving her hand. "Let him sleep all day." She goes down the hall to the closet and starts crinkling through the bags and paper she's saved.

I look at the rock. I touch it with my fingertips and imagine the hand—the white hand—that threw it. My stomach quivers, and I take my fingers off. Rhonda walks over, takes the rock, and drops it into the waste bag with the broken glass. The fragments tinkle. And Rhonda walks out, glancing down at me that way, so erect. "So Luke," I hear her think, "you've finally come awake, haven't you? This is what it took." And I am awake, I guess, though not in the way she probably thinks.

Leaning the broom against the wall, I bend down and carefully retrieve the rock, then hold it tightly with both hands in my lap. I squeeze it. I want to crush it. My mother has found a big piece of wrapping paper and is unfolding it. She gets some tape from a drawer and is getting ready to cover the window when my father walks in. He stands there blinking, husky and rumpled in his

5

blue bathrobe. Mom looks at him, lips parted. His mouth opens, his eyes narrow, and he's just staring at the glass teeth. "Oh jeez," he mutters. His shoulders sink a little. I watch the creases around his mouth. My father worked hard to move us here.

Time is suspended before me — Dad's eyes fastened on the window, Mom looking at him. And from nowhere comes an inner tug as I'm struck by how purely, suddenly, they are themselves. Dad's stare is the stare of his life, the essence of the one he trains on the world each day — twin cores of light, deep in smoke. His brow bunches in a frown. At his sides hang the webbed hands that have dug a thousand ditches. And Mom watches him, gathering herself to meet the hard-pressed spirit she knows so well, to soothe it with soft words.

"I just got done with the police," she says. "They said — "

"There it is!" Rhonda calls from the living room. "There's our official welcome to Flower Heights!"

I feel like telling Rhonda to shut her mouth, but instead I hide the rock in my hands while my father stands there and Mom starts taping the paper to the pane.

"I'll fix it tomorrow," I hear myself say.

And I'm thinking about tomorrow. Tomorrow at school.

September 28th

Rhonda and I stand with Nate Chisholm at the bus stop. The white kids stand in a knot a few yards away, speaking low and chuckling a little. Bus comes. The driver's a taciturn man with a pasty round face and hardly ever looks at anyone as they get on. I sit with Nate; he says he heard about our window and that his father is having trouble with a white neighbor. Also, his older brother got roughed up by two white guys at the drugstore.

I met Nate the first day of school. His family moved here shortly before us, and his folks were over for dinner once. Nate's a shy kid, awkward. And now he's worried, eyes wide as he speaks in a near-whisper. Worried about the whole picture, but especially about this neighbor who has threatened to shoot his father.

"This guy, he's not screwed on right," he says. "He was out in his driveway screaming over at my father, and I couldn't hardly tell what he was saying."

I can't think of anything to say, so I let Nate talk.

"This guy, he's just crazy. And my father's got a temper."

The bus makes two more stops. A dozen or so white

kids get on, and five black ones. Wilbur Shaw gets on at the last stop, wearing the long leather coat he keeps on all day, and sits beside Rhonda. As Nate talks I look back and Rhonda's telling Wilbur about the incident, the hard sharpness in her face matching his. Wilbur is with Nate and me in U.S. history class, where he sits up front looking bored but still talks a lot — sometimes interrupting Mr. McBride — and uses big words, often in the wrong way. He's also in my gym class; he's good at basketball.

The school is a block away now, and Nate is quiet. I'm thinking of McBride's class, in which we have a test today. That's my favorite class, mostly because of McBride.

"You all set for that history test?" I ask Nate.

He puts his hand to his mouth. "Shit, I forgot all about it!"

As we pull up to the school I'm trying to tell Nate all the stuff he'll have to know for the test, firing it off to him.

Angus T. Bently High School is a big building of yellow brick, with deep-set windows that gather shadow. As we stride toward the doors we fall silent, watching an old janitor wash three red spray-paint words from the 1963 cornerstone. The latter two are squeezed too tightly to read, but the first is "niggers."

The buzz of homeroom after roll call — more subdued this morning. About a week after school started, the voluntary seating that split each classroom down the middle

—black side, white side—began to crumble inward. This place was actually starting to feel easier. Then the trouble hit and the order snapped back hard, running clean as a blade down the center aisle—black side, white side. So here I am, on the black side.

Mr. Irwin, dapper and unsmiling, scribbles at his desk. I stare at the blank blackboard and, to kill time, run through the chronology in my head. In late July there was the melee at that bar in the city. The cops said it started when bottles were thrown at them when they arrived to quell a fight. Another version was that the police got heavy-handed before the big trouble started. What's certain is that it nearly became a riot. Eight injuries, a dozen arrests (mostly black), and the bar burned out. That was several days before we moved here—just a four-mile hop to the outskirts, though that's hard to grasp.

Since then there's been a firecracker string of incidents in the city. I can honestly say I'm glad to be in Flower Heights now, glad I'm at Bently instead of Randolph, where things are worse. The thought of Randolph—the dark stone, the bashed-in lockers, and the smell of the halls—makes me queasy.

Yeah, it was feeling easier shortly after school opened here. The anxiety had settled to a low, cool pulse, under control. That changed two weeks ago—a long time, it seems. Two Mondays ago, the curse came to roost. The night before, a black guy and a white guy had gotten into a fight outside the 7-Eleven, and the white had been stabbed. Before the day ended a black freshman had been beaten, down by the playing field; he's still in the hospital. Suddenly the eyes of white kids I passed in the hall

11

lost the hazy truce of indifference; their glances became glares. A girl would quicken her steps. A guy's hands would clench at his sides. And I became aware of an ache, as if circuits had shorted beneath my skin, and I couldn't finish my lunches. The Friday before last a black bus-in kid from the city, George Law, got into a fight with a Flower Heights native named Andy Crown. Crown took the worst of it before Mr. Lattanzio wrenched them apart. Both were suspended. They're in my history class too.

I try to recall these incidents as dispassionately as I can, but each is like the jab of a stick. Over to my right, someone says that during the weekend, police collared a kid who they think called in the two bomb scares last week. Then behind me someone mutters that Law and Crown are back. That ache is back too, under my skin — and a hint of nausea. The first bell is a relief, sort of.

I hold my books tightly to my hip and walk fast, not looking at anyone. The halls are filled with a dead gray light. No bashed-in lockers here, but it suddenly looks a lot like Randolph.

In English, Mrs. Rollins is reading to us from Stephen Crane's "The Blue Hotel." She finishes the passage with a flourish and holds the book out, gesturing at it with the other chubby hand. "So you see, in his terror to avoid death, the Swede actually *brings about* his death. There's a lot of irony at work here." Her lips twitch into a sweet smile. She's a short blond lady with lively blue eyes that flicker delight over good stories, stories with tricky hidden designs. She loves them.

12

But I notice that the book quivers in her hand. Another thing I've noticed is that she has skipped a story in the book—Dreiser's "Nigger Jim."

"But the Swede . . . the Swede has help in this," she goes on. "The other men unknowingly contribute to his fate. Can anyone tell me how?"

Silence. At these monents I usually take pity and raise my hand. Not this time, though the pity's there. Instead I escape into a reverie I often have, on the question of what kind of guy I am and what I'll end up doing with my life.

I have what qualifies as a cynical streak; I take some things too seriously; I like most kids and dogs; while smart enough, I'm not as smart as I wanted to be; I'm an aspiring healer of some kind, with a fair-sized ego waiting in the wings. When I was twelve or so, I had this fantasy about reigning as a folksy benevolent king over a realm of loving subjects. These days, though graduation still seems a light-year off, I imagine myself alternately as a doctor, a lawyer, and a writer. We'll see.

At the end of class Mrs. Rollins stops me at the door, smiling, and hands me back the story I wrote, with an A-plus on it. "It was so good, Luke. You really captured Crane's style."

"Thank you," I tell her.

This was one of the whimsical assignments she's prone to give—a story written in the manner of Crane. It was fun to do. It's about an ex-slave fighting in the Civil War, and frankly, I think the style turned out more mine than Crane's (not to knock Crane).

In math class, Mr. Irwin's chalk-dust drone is for once a refuge and not a weight on my brain. I fade into the swirl of equations, reaching further and further into them as his chalk taps like a telegraph. But halfway through, during one of Irwin's minute-long silences, this fails me. My insides slump. What I'd rather hear is the warm rhythm of McBride's voice, never thinning into silence. But in history, today of all days, it's a test instead of a regular class.

Study period in the library—Nate locked into his history book, me skimming mine, while Mrs. Hoffmann stands guard over the crowded tables. One thing about Mrs. Hoffman, the thing that separates her from the other teachers, is that when you look at her, you get the message. She's tall and thin, her graying hair tied back, and she stares through glasses you figure she must have been born wearing. She'd be pretty attractive if not for the hard jaw. The glasses, folded arms, and straight back say it all. I have her for Spanish.

Over in one corner there's whispering, then a fluttery laugh; I crane my neck and it's Jennie Davis, slouched in her chair. She's a bus-in, a straight-ahead ghetto kid with unusually big eyes. She's wearing the tattered green top she had on the first day of school. The sight of her then got me hot enough—until she opened her mouth. She's in McBride's class also. Someone told me she's crazy. And to Mrs. Hoffmann, at the moment, her laughter is an enemy beachhead.

Jennie holds a half-smile as Hoffmann comes over with slow steps, arms still folded. Everyone's watching.

"We don't need that, Jennie," she says calmly.

"Wuz wrong with it?" Jennie shrugs.

Hoffmann's stare gleams down. "You're disturbing the other people."

"Wasn't disturbing nobody. Nothin' wrong with a little laugh."

Jennie's friends titter. Hoffmann stands there like a ghost, letting a silent moment pass. "If you keep it up," she says, "you can go tell Mr. O'Donnell there's nothing wrong with it."

Hoffmann turns and, without a backward glance, returns to her post by the counter. Jennie smirks across at her friends, then widens those big eyes in a mock glower and crosses her arms. Someone chuckles.

From a nearby table, George Law and his friends cast long looks at the girls. Law is thickset in his black T-shirt, one arm slung over the chair back. There's a scab on his forehead.

Old Mrs. Wells, the librarian, fidgets with a file drawer. Then the bell sounds and we get out.

In history, Nate sits to my left, still reading. Wilbur Shaw is a couple of seats ahead and to the right, looking bored. Far to my right, on the other side, is Andy Crown —a muscular, shaggy kid with his sleeves rolled up and a faded bruise on his face. He wears a sort of leer as three other white guys talk to him in a hushed, eager way. In the back of the room are the bus-in kids. Jennie prattles to Law about Hoffmann. Law sits with his legs stretched into both aisles. The kids around him are turned in their seats, listening to Jennie but watching Law attentively. Like most of the bus-ins, Law was plucked from Culver High, across town. He arrived here with a certain reputation about him, not to mention the small squad of hangers-on. After class not long ago he said to me, "You so smart, I wanna be just like you when I grow up."

Then McBride walks in, carrying a folder of test sheets. He stands behind his desk, rearranging books and papers as the low hum of voices continues.

Since it's been only three weeks, I still don't know him very well. But something made me respect him right off. I guess it's this air of solidity he has. It doesn't come from the neatness of his tweed jacket—Irwin is a sharper dresser, but he's still Irwin. Rather, it's the self-assurance in McBride's movements. They're straight, easy movements, seldom quick, even when he's just turning a page or raising his forefinger to make a point, or when his hands come up to his hips as he paces. It fits well with his slimness and a fine-featured face that's youthful except for eye wrinkles and gray sideburns. He's in his early thirties, I'd say. He's one of four black teachers at Bently, not counting Mrs. Jessup, the vice-principal. His skin is light, lighter than mine. I overheard one kid say McBride's father was white; someone else said it was his mother, and added that he was divorced.

His class is as much a haven as I've found in this place. From the first he was friendly to me, having picked me out as one of the less conspicuous ones, and he gives a nod-and-smile each time he sees me. The way he teaches —it's like he summons the figures and events, assembles them with care and without too much digression, and then lets them march. And sometimes—twice a week maybe—he even drops a joke: The Boston Tea party happened because the town was just as drunk on weekends back then as it is now . . . In 1776, the slaves thought, "Wow, now we can wear chains in a free country instead of in a colony!" When he's speaking, he paces from the map stand to the window and back, his gaze level. Even Jennie shuts up for him.

One day last week, before I went home, I came back to his room to get a notebook I'd forgotten. McBride was there, talking to a white girl named Holly Cliff who's my lab partner in chemistry. There were tears on her face. I gave a clumsy "Excuse me" and got the notebook from under my desk; McBride continued talking to her in a subdued tone. As I left I heard Holly laugh at something he said; it was the sudden, uneven giggle of someone unused to laughter. In homeroom the next day, I overheard something about Holly's parents splitting up.

So I like McBride.

He has opened the folder and is skimming over a test copy. Look up, McBride. Say, "Okay, folks." That's how he begins, always.

McBride looks up, and my gut tightens again. His eyes dart among the faces before him. He's frowning. Without a word, he takes out the sheaf of tests and a stack of blue books and begins moving down the aisles, putting one of each on each desk. Nate puts his book away and the voices dissolve. I glance up at McBride as he places a test and a blue book on my desk, but he doesn't look at me. He moves past me and I'm looking at the test, seeing the letters but not the words. Usually he says, "Hi, Luke."

"You gave me two," a white guy says.

Silently McBride takes back the extra sheet and finishes distributing the others. Then he sits at his desk. I look at him once more, then write my name on the blue book. Fifteen multiple-choice questions, two essays.

*   *   *

17

In the cafeteria I sit with Nate. Lunch is tuna burgers, and I'm having trouble getting it down. Nate's going on about the test.

"It was hard, but I think I might've done okay. I don't think those essays were fair, did you?"

"Wasn't easy," I mumble. But really it was easy enough.

I wish it were easy not to look two tables away, where Rhonda is sitting with Wilbur and some friends of his. Wilbur's friends are mostly kids from other black families who've moved out here in the past year or so. A couple are bus-ins, but all of them are better-dressed than the average kid. Wilbur's father, I've heard, runs a couple of stores downtown, one of which was damaged by fire last month.

Right now Wilbur is talking intently to Rhonda, gesturing with open hands above his tray. They're seated together in the middle, and the others listen closely, with serious faces, nodding. Rhonda nods decisively and speaks. Her voice is sharp and I catch her words. "That's right, that's right, a conspiracy. One way or another you end up with some kind of ghetto. Doesn't matter where you are." Wilbur nods, just as decisively.

I suck slowly on my milk straw. The ghettos—what would Rhonda do without them? What would she have to talk about that wouldn't bore her, and where would she get her social theories, glazed in outrage? I think that deep down she loves them—or, more rightly, the thought of them, the picture.

Rhonda once did a painting in art class; she's a very good artist. It showed a street in Harlem with brown-and-yellow tenements and people working, talking, and walking. A rich, busy painting—bright, dark, and alive. I think it's still hanging in her bedroom.

Rhonda and I have never lived in an actual ghetto, as Mom and Dad once did. Uncle Earl and his family live in one, in Pittsburgh, and I'm reminded now of the last time we all visited them, the summer before last. A small incident occurred with Rhonda during that visit—one of the very few times I've seen her off-balance and exposed.

Just before we left, she and I were out on the steps of the building, waiting for Mom and Dad to come down. We were out there because our cousin, Earl Jr., was too much to take. He's a fat, loud kid who makes fun of how I talk (Mr. Education, he calls me) even though I don't say much around him, and who always acts hot over Rhonda. We were sitting there, not saying anything, and the smell of garbage was drifting down the street. Then Rhonda got up and walked over to the car, I suppose to get in and continue waiting. She was opening the door when two older dudes came walking around the corner, and their heads turned as they passed her.

"Hey, fancy," one said.

Rhonda paused with her hand on the door. Instantly they halted, grinning at her.

"What you doin' here with that fancy dress, babe?" said the taller one.

"Yeah," said the other. "You think you uptown with all them white folks?"

She blinked at them.

"I know!" said the tall one. "The lady's lost."

He stepped up to her and put his hand on her arm. "I can take you where you wanna go, babe. Uptown with all them white folks struttin' around."

I rose to my feet, and the other one noticed me. He leered up at me. "Hey, man. She yours?"

Just then Mom and Dad appeared in the doorway. The shorter one tapped his friend on the shoulder. "Come on, Eddie. We got a plane to catch, man."

Seeing Dad, the taller one took his hand off Rhonda. "Oh yeah! Yeah, we gotta get goin'." He smiled, and they headed down the sidewalk.

"Bye-bye!" the shorter one yelled, waving.

"See y'all at the country club!" called the other.

Dad stared darkly after them, and Mom looked down at Rhonda. "What was that all about?" she asked.

Rhonda didn't answer, just stared after the two guys. And she hardly said anything on the long drive home. After looking out the window a while, she curled up and dozed off.

I hate the ghettos. I hate the garbage smell, and the screams of playing children send a cold sting through my bones. Most of all I hate the buildings with their peeling paint, the lonely flower boxes, the windows with ragged curtains and sometimes a face staring down. That's why any picture I'd ever paint of the ghetto would be nothing like Rhonda's.

"Luke?"

I look at Nate and stop sucking on my straw. His fragile look is gone; his eyes are hot.

"Did you see Andy Crown? You see him sitting there in class like he's a big shit?" His voice is hushed and hard.

"Yeah, I saw him."

"I'd like to bust that motherfucker's head."

20

Like I said, Nate's a shy kid, and not big or tough-looking. I can't think of a reply, so I nod instead.

"I'd like to waste his white ass," Nate hisses.

I leave one of the tuna burgers uneaten.

Going to chemistry class, I meet McBride, who stops me with a hand on my shoulder. "Luke, I looked your essays over," he says. "They're just what I wanted." He's smiling now.

"Thanks." I nod, and he strides on past. I suddenly feel better.

Mr. Walker is a balding, big-shouldered guy who, when he's not holding chalk or a pointer or a beaker, clasps both hands behind him. He talks with his head tipped back slightly, as if to make his voice come from further up. I don't know why, because he's tall enough.

I haven't liked him since the day he handed me back a lab report with these words: "Luke, you got a C on this because I've seen your IQ scores. Ideally, you'd be in an accelerated program, and if you were, you'd get a C or worse for this."

Chemistry isn't my academic ace, and Mr. Walker isn't my favorite person. Right now we're in pairs, doing an experiment while Walker does his walking, hands behind him — a slow roll from station to station, like a ship's captain.

Holly, my lab partner, hands me a graduated cylinder, and I start pouring in saline solution from a beaker.

Holly is smart and really pretty, dark-haired, with a penchant for striped sweaters. She's also a nice kid, it seems, though I'm still a little awkward around her. I was sorry to hear about her parents breaking up. I thought she might be embarrassed about my blundering onto that scene with McBride last week, but she doesn't seem to be.

"How much is that again?" I ask.

"Six point five," she says.

I stop pouring and use the dropper to get the rest in.

"Okay?" she asks.

"Close enough," I say, and too late I notice Walker behind me.

"No such thing as 'close enough' in chemistry, Luke," he intones. "Check that again."

I draw a bit of the solution out with a dropper, and Walker moves on. Holly gives me a wry smile.

"Captain Bligh," I mutter.

She nods. "He used to be a navy man."

"Figures. How do you know that?"

"My mom's on the school board," she says. "She knows some of the teachers."

Lately Holly's eyes have been puffy and she's talked less. But today her spirits appear high. There are moments, though, when she seems to be straining. I wonder what's behind that smile.

Just then this white guy, a jock named Chuck Cameron, comes up behind Holly and squirts her with his water bottle.

"Chuck!" she squeals.

Returning to his station, he grins over at her, and she half-smiles. "You jerk!"

"That's cute, Chuck." Walker speaks gravely. "None of that, okay?"

22

Holly smiles at me, kind of embarrassed, and shrugs. "What next?"

"The acid, I think." And as I look down to check the workbook, I catch Cameron glancing over at us. It's only for an instant, but it stays with me for the rest of the period, stinking like the acid—that sullen mouth, edging on a sneer. For a moment I feel vague hate for that face, but soon there's only fatigue, pressing down.

I drag the tiredness to Spanish class, where I sit in the back and barely hear Mrs. Hoffmann. Once when she calls on me I fumble through my book and give the wrong answer. The girl behind me answers right, and as I sink back into the haze, I can't help noting how doggedly the same Hoffmann always is, how straight her back, how even the step of those pencil legs. If I weren't so tired, I might even be amazed, or envious of this thin white woman. But I am tired. Christ I'm tired, and it's only Monday.

Ever since school started I've walked home. Today I consider waiting for the three o'clock bus, but I want to be home so much that it's only a passing thought. Carrying my books, I leave through the front and pass the cornerstone with the pale red stain where the graffiti were. As I near the sidewalk, I find myself checking in all directions—ahead, behind me, all around.

Almost by reflex I take a deep breath when I reach the sidewalk. The sky's still gray, and the trees, with leaves turning orange, seem out of place as they rustle. Home —push homeward.

Then I see a couple ambling along up ahead, and it's

Rhonda and Wilbur. I hear them talking softly as I gain on them. Passing Rhonda, I nod hello.

"Hi, Luke," says Wilbur.

"Hi," Rhonda says, barely. She resumes talking in a low voice as I move beyond them.

I forget when or why the trouble betweeen Rhonda and me started. It doesn't seem we've ever been close, though I know we were close enough as kids. She was a happy kid, though prone to tantrums. We fought a lot, but no more than you'd expect. Sometimes I think I must have done something wrong, way back. With each year Rhonda spent more time drawing pictures in her room, passing from crayons to paint, kid themes to social themes. The time came when she seemed embarrassed to run into me at school and started looking at me as if I didn't fit into the epic-filled world she saw; I was an obstacle, an uninvited guest. I've never asked her about it, and she volunteers little. I did ask Mom once, and she said it was normal.

The streets of neat houses pass quickly. A big white car glides by, then a police cruiser, and I catch a glance from the cop inside. A middle-aged white woman eyes me from her porch. Nothing unusual, of course, but I'm still not fond of it. Nearing home, I pass a group of little white kids playing in a driveway. They go silent, watching me.

"Hey, brother! What's happenin'?" one little boy calls with a lisp.

"Not much," I say. "What's happenin' with you?"

The kids giggle.

As I turn down my street, all the houses and trim yards

seem locked against me. The windows watch me go by.

I'm almost home when I pass a pot-bellied man in a flowered shirt—the one who was mowing his lawn yesterday. His eyes snap to one side when he sees me coming.

"Hi," I mumble. No reply. Why'd I bother?

When I come in the door, Mom has just come in from hanging clothes. Her expression is preoccupied, misty, but she smiles. Almost always she smiles.

"Hi, dear. How was today?"

"Was okay," I tell her.

"Good. You going to fix the window?"

The window. I rub my eyes and go to the kitchen. There it still is, waiting for me. She's taken the paper off.

"Daddy said he'd have the new pane with him when he gets home," she tells me.

I'm inclined to put such things off till tomorrow, but not this time. I move the kitchen table over, then get gloves and a hammer and a chisel from the cellar and go to work. While Mom cooks dinner I chop at the putty, big shards of glass dropping around my sneakers. I hear Rhonda come in the door and go upstairs. I keep at it, and all the time I'm thinking, "I'm getting rid of you, you ugly bastard. Momma's gonna have her view back." When the glass is all on the floor, I gather it in paper bags and take it to the garage, just as Dad's car pulls into the driveway.

I call hello as he gets out. His work pants are caked with dirt in places. Dad's a supervisor with the city's largest landscaping firm.

"Hi, Luke," he says, kind of absently. I see that yesterday's look is still on him—that distant, tight-lipped look. I tell him the window's ready and he says, "Good." Carefully we take the new pane from the back of the car and bring it inside.

Mom's stew smells good, but supper is delayed as we place the pane and putty it in. Afterward, as evening darkens, we stand back, and it looks fine. I feel satisfied. Mom looks out, then gives me a smile. Rhonda sweeps the area, and we move the table back before washing up.

Dad, Rhonda, and I hardly talk over dinner, so it's mostly left to Mom. She asks Dad about work, and he tells about a man who got fired today for being drunk on the job. Mom tells what she saw on Phil Donahue. Then, right out of the blue, Rhonda mentions the graffiti at school.

Mom stops eating. "God." She sighs, then looks at me. "You didn't mention *that*."

"Didn't you see it?" Rhonda asks, almost glaring.

"Yeah." I nod. "I saw it."

Hunched over his plate, Dad gives a low grunt.

Later I'm in my room doing homework. On some impulse I get up and go downstairs. I pass through the living room, where Mom and Dad are watching TV, his arm resting on her shoulders. In the kitchen, I stand looking through the window into the gloom. Then I go out and sit on the porch, slouched against the door. Lawn lamps shine as elms rustle, and the breeze is cool.

September 29th

Shaw sits with Rhonda on the bus again this morning. He's his talkative self, all firm stares and open-handed gestures. Rhonda's attentive, with her own firm stare. I don't hear what he's talking about and I don't care. Nate dozes beside me. I'm hoping I can slip through this day without two things—a white sneer, and the sound of Wilbur Shaw.

In gym an hour and a half later I'm shooting baskets while Mr. Lattanzio prowls watchfully on the sides, his whistle dangling. He allows us to do pretty much what we want, as long as he can keep an eye on us. Lattanzio is a cliché gym teacher, your basic barrel-chested, bellowing ex-Marine.

At the far end, some guys are well into a game of basketball. Two of them are black, and that gives me a slight feeling of comfort. Under the hoop, at least, you can sweat your way out of the war zone, forget it for a while and not care about the color of whoever you're guarding.

I shoot and miss, shoot and miss again. I've never gotten the magic in my arms that sends the ball into the arc-and-swish. Usually this annoys me, but now I'm just glad to be by myself.

Trying to get a shot from the side, I notice a white kid named Barry McLeod step onto the floor and stand there, looking around kind of nervously. He's in my Spanish class, where he sits way back—a messy-haired, ordinary-looking kid whose manner reminds me of Nate. I've played basketball with him a few times but have never really spoken to him.

Then he sees me, and I bounce the ball to him.

"Thanks," he says quietly, and shoots. He misses. Barry's arms have no more magic than mine.

I sink one from the foul line.

"Nice," he says.

"How'd you do with that translation for Hoffmann?" I ask, passing him the ball.

Smiling, he shakes his head. "I used the dictionary a lot."

As Barry shoots I hear another ball bouncing behind me. I look and it's Wilbur, primed for a long shot.

"Hey, Luke," he says.

"Hello."

Aside from yesterday, I can't remember Wilbur ever greeting me before. His shot snaps perfectly through the net.

"Nice shot," Barry says. Wilbur doesn't look at him, just tenses with the ball again. He lets it go as Barry shoots, and the balls collide above the hoop.

"Sorry," Barry mutters.

Wilbur's ball bounces to me and I hand it to him. "Thanks," he says. "How you been doing?"

Barry is walking away.

"All right," I answer.

30

"No hard times with Mr. Whitey?"

"Not yet."

Wilbur's ball swishes again. "Try a shot," he tells me.

I try it and miss.

"Rhonda told me about your window," Wilbur says.

"Yeah, we fixed it," I tell him.

"None of us is totally safe," he says gravely. "Specially not here. I decided I'm gonna get a knife."

I shrug. "Hide it good."

"Sure I'll hide it, but I'll bring it out when it comes to be necessary. It's survival, man."

His next shot goes in off the backboard. Catching the ball, he holds it at his hip and makes a fist. "We all gotta stick together. Like real brothers."

I look at his sneakers and shrug again. "Sure."

He starts bouncing the ball again. "They're trying to make niggers out of us, just like always. Some ways are direct, others are indirect. But they're trying, man."

He shoots and misses off the rim.

"They're good at throwing rocks," I mutter.

"What we all gotta do is continue to hang tough," he goes on, drumming the ball at his knees. "We gotta say no, just like Huey Newton and the others did. I been reading stuff from the sixties, by Newton and Cleaver and other ones."

I put my hands out and he gives me the ball. Concentrating on the hoop, I try to think I'm alone. The ball bounces in.

"That's what gave me an idea," he continues. "I'm starting a Black Students' Defense League." He sinks one from the line, then holds the ball to his hip again. "I talked to Rhonda about it, and she says she'll help me. We could walk home in groups, demand more protection—all that kind of thing."

I nod. "Uh-huh."

"First I gotta talk it up," he says. "You could really contribute, help talk it up."

Lattanzio's whistle pierces the gym. "All right, let's go!" he hollers. "Roll the balls in!"

Wilbur does a lay-up, then bounces the ball away. "Think about it, Luke. Talk it up to Nate Chisholm and anybody else, okay? I could use you."

I nod. "Okay."

He glances back as though he expects me to follow, then heads for the showers.

The ball I began with has rolled up to my toes, and I pick it up. Black Students' Defense League—such an official ring, I think. So ideal, as a mantle of importance, for a guy like Wilbur. But what digs at me is that the idea is probably a good one, at bottom. If things keep up, maybe there will be no alternative but that or something like it. And at least Wilbur, for his part, is moving in some clear direction. I shoot and miss.

Suddenly I'm frustrated. Why do I always think too much? I know I'm madder and more scared than I've ever been, and that's all. Granted, I've never been in a spot like this before, but if Wilbur and Rhonda can be decisive and confusion-free, preparing for action in their own ways, why can't I? I envy them—so much I can taste it. I envy them for their hard-edged vision of struggle, which holds them upright like a metal spine. And I envy their flashing, immediate sense of history—different from mine, different from McBride's, somehow more rooted in the recent past—a romantic continuum of which they and the events here are so snugly a part. Their imaginations lie with the Black Panthers and marching feet, mine with Frederick Douglass and the Emancipation. That's a time distant enough for me to feel comfortable with and to romp around in when I daydream. What all this says about me and about Rhonda and Wilbur, I'm not sure. What matters is that with their anger comes heroic inspiration.

Inspiration. The last time I could say I was inspired was last year, when Jesse Jackson visited Randolph. The auditorium was packed, but everyone was silent as his voice went *clong clang clong*, echoing off every corner like a brimstone bell. Then there was the chant—him standing up there, fist raised, and all of us on our feet. And the final words: "You may not be responsible for being down, but you *are* responsible for *getting back up!*" I recall thinking that the ceiling would fall as I beat my hands together, buried in the roar. My skin didn't just tingle—it buzzed. I wonder if it would today. I wonder, because the whole memory feels sealed off like a dream I half-remember.

"Parrish!" Lattanzio barks. "Are you asleep?"

As I go in, my mind untangles: there's got to be something besides just being angry and scared. Wilbur's working on his way of facing the music. And if I'm not going to be absorbed by his or anyone else's solution, I sure as hell better come up with my own. A better one, if possible, and soon. My handicap is that I have no overview, no knack for that useful mental separation of people into camps and causes, good and bad, for and against. Where Wilbur and Rhonda, from the perch of their convictions, see warring bands and warring flags, I just see small individuals—one here, one there; one to like, another to dislike. Still, I'm bound with every other black kid in this school by the basic question, how to deal with whites as the days get uglier?

In the mildewed damp of the locker room, I'm undressing when I hear a voice from over near the showers: "Get the fuck outa my way!"

I go still, to listen, and then there's wet scuffling and shouts.

"Get your fuckin' hands off me!" another voice yells. It's Wilbur.

"I'll kick you to shit!"

Quickly I peer around the lockers, and Wilbur's there, facing this white guy named Mark Toohey whom I've seen with Andy Crown a lot. They're both naked, dripping, their towels at their feet. Each has his fists clenched. It's just the whites standing around. One black guy stands beyond them, clutching his towel. Then he slips out through the corridor to the gym. Barry stares from a corner.

"Waste his ass, Mark!" yells a fat, moon-faced white.

Wilbur stiffens as Toohey takes a small step forward. "Better watch it, you black bastard!"

I take two strides toward them and stop cold, staring at Wilbur's tight, lean face.

Lattanzio storms in. "What in Jesus is going on?" he bellows, shoving Toohey aside. He glares at the two of them, then grabs both by their bare shoulders. "Are you crazy?'' he shouts. ''Are you both loose in the head?''

Out in the hall the bell rings, but everyone remains, staring.

''He shoved me in the shower!'' Wilbur nearly whines.

''Bullshit!'' Toohey sneers.

Lattanzio shakes them. ''I don't care! I don't care who . . . '' He turns to the onlookers. ''All of you get to class!''

I haven't moved since taking those two steps. And I haven't taken a shower yet. I sit on the bench as the others finish dressing and file out quickly. Lattanzio orders Wilbur and Toohey to dress fast and come with him to the office. I don't look up as they pass by, and Lattanzio doesn't notice me. ''Stupid!'' he's shouting. ''I could kick you both in the butt!''

I can't move quickly, though I know I'll be late for class. In the trickling quiet of the showers I feel the water running down, so cool, and wish I could stay here until the last bell.

I'm five minutes late for McBride's class. On the way there I have this sensation that the floor is slipping away beneath my feet; I have to look down at the flecked surface to make sure it's solid.

McBride is half-leaning, half-sitting on his desk when I come in, and he doesn't break off from his monologue. I take my seat beside Nate.

''So,'' McBride says, ''although Locke and Rousseau were gurus of the Revolution, Paine was the one who was around for it, who actually served in the Continental Army.''

For the first time since I heard the shout in the locker room, I begin to relax. This time McBride looks and sounds as he should up there—calm, his cadence intact. Yesterday he was a little off. And shouldn't he be allowed that, once in a while? Was I expecting him to be Iron Man? Once again he's an island for me, pacing to the window.

"Paine's name was appropriate because he was a pain in the side of authority wherever he went. And that included . . ."

Wilbur arrives. He hands McBride a "late" slip and drops into his seat. McBride flicks the slip onto his desk and goes on.

"That included America after the Revolution. Basically, the men who made the war wanted the British tax men off their backs. They liked the idea of independence, but they had no use for an idealist such as Paine, once he'd served his purpose." He picks up his textbook and turns through it with careful fingers.

Wilbur's practiced boredom seems ruffled; tight around the mouth, he slowly scratches one knee.

"But all that came after," McBride says. "Here's what Paine wrote at the Revolution's darkest hour: 'These are the times that try men's souls . . . The summer soldier and the sunshine patriot will, in this crisis, shrink from the service of his country; but he that stands it now—' "

Wilbur's voice stabs up. "What good does it do—"

"Save it till I'm finished, Wilbur," says McBride, and reads on. " 'Tyranny, like hell, is not easily conquered; yet we have this consolation with us, that the harder the

36

conflict, the more glorious the triumph. What we obtain too cheap, we esteem too lightly. . . ' "

Almost everyone's looking at Wilbur. McBride finishes reading, places the book back on the desk, and gestures to him.

"What's the purpose of reading this stuff?" Wilbur says. Holding the comment apparently strengthened its poison—it comes out almost as a spit. The room is still.

McBride folds his arms, buttresslike, and blinks down at Wilbur. "The purpose of it? Don't you think there's some value in learning how we got from there to here?"

Wilbur's hand grips his knee. "That thing—that thing you were just reading. What good is that to us?"

"It lets us see the spirit that fanned the fire," McBride says quickly. "And because it's an inspiration for—"

"Did any of that come true?" Wilbur glares, flicking his palm at McBride. "Any of that stuff in there, or anything in the Declaration of Independence?"

Someone in back giggles. And Jennie Davis is mimicking Wilbur's hand motions, as she often has—can't let this get too heavy, after all.

McBride places his hands behind him. "That's not the point," he says. "He's talking about an ideal."

"What about the slaves?" Wilbur says. "You talked about that yourself!"

"Right." McBride nods. "These things proceed in stages. It took another war to take care of that matter."

"Yeah, for what?" Wilbur shoots back, spreading his palms. Jennie spreads hers.

"For what?" McBride says. "Well, I haven't picked any cotton today, have you?"

37

Laughter springs. From me, and from all around. McBride smiles at Wilbur, who's ebony-hard, looking down.

"And as for the lighter-complected folks here, I haven't seen any of them eating pecans on the verandah." That's it, McBride — go with the momentum. "You see, Wilbur, the present never looks good when you're smack dab in the middle of it." He taps the textbook. "*This* lifts you up out of it so you can see . . ."

Wilbur looks up, and McBride's smile fades. "How long?" Wilbur says, his bottom teeth showing. "How long do we just go by reading stuff like that? That book doesn't do a goddamn thing for me. It's shit."

Quiet again. McBride folds his arms again, thinking. He paces to the blackboard and turns. "If you think it's shit . . . then I guess it's my job to change your mind." He paces back to the desk. His face has changed. He's frowning now, with a look as sullen as Wilbur's. "But I'm telling you this. However things are now . . ." For a moment he looks toward this side of the room, but at no one in particular; eyes must look that way in the dark. "It's a stage," he says. "Like any other time."

Then his voice lifts and the frown snaps away. "The Revolution was a stage, during which the whole concept of individual rights took a big leap ahead. . . "

For the rest of the period I don't really listen. When the bell rings, Wilbur is the first to leave. Nate gives me that wide-eyed, worried glance as we go out the door. And when I look back I see McBride in his chair, chin in his hand.

*   *   *

38

Nate and I lose each other and I eat lunch alone. The lectures in chemistry and Spanish pass in a blur.

Walking home, I'm thinking of Wilbur's little outburst, wondering what it was about it that nags me. For a moment there, Wilbur nearly summoned the black-and-white monster. Wilbur, the one who loves the sound of his own voice, the grim politico whom I don't particularly like. For that crackling moment the floorboards split and the monster peeked at us from beneath—biding his time, possibly. But aside from that obvious fear, there was something else. In his flailing, Wilbur bumped a hornet's nest inside me that I'd forgotten was there. I felt the anger start to swarm from it, thick and throbbing with the deep drone of wings—anger at fate, at whites, at myself, and yes, at the stately pronouncements on liberty that sounded so fine when McBride spoke them. As Wilbur went on, I felt his words dragging me away, beyond his guerrilla strut, beyond the reach of McBride's wisdom and the ideals of history, to a place that's cold and dark, where bitterness eats and eats you. It's a place I've known and dreaded, and different things have taken me there.

The first time was two Christmases ago. I still don't know exactly what brought it on, just that one gray day in my room, with nothing to do, I realized I didn't like the person I was. At school they were calling me "Megabrain" and giving me a hard time in gym. I was nervous with girls, and my face looked ugly in the mirror. I wasn't interested in much anymore and had started to get the first inkling that I wasn't necessarily going to be the one who'd end strife or cure cancer. Reviewing all this, I felt myself falling down a shaft, down to the cold, dark place. This continued for a week, through the shine of tree ornaments, the carols, and the crinkly ribboned paper, during which I questioned whether happiness was realistic and life worth my effort. I went for long walks past grimy snowbanks or stayed in my room, where I fantasized about exploding, just going up like a stack of dynamite. Other times I imagined sinking so low that my heart would simply stop.

In time Mom and Dad noticed I hadn't been saying much. Mom prodded but didn't press. It all culminated in an argument with Rhonda over what to watch on TV. Upstairs, I put my fist through the plaster by my bed. Dad, who'd been giving me bewildered glances, reacted in the only way he knew; he got mad. "What the hell's the matter with him?" I overheard him saying to Mom. "It's Christmas!" When Mom quietly asked me about it, I told her, with a dry throat, and added that I'd fix the wall. Rhonda's whole attitude was a bemused shrug; I recall hating her for a while. Back at school I was still Megabrain, but with less time to think I started feeling better.

Since then, though, I haven't liked Christmas. And since then there've been other times. This past spring a girl named Melinda guessed that I had hopes about her and turned icy on me, touching off another period — a month this time — of tight silence, questioning, hibernation, and bloody movies in my head. At such times I come home and turn the stereo up loud. Dad looks confused and impatient and shakes his head a lot. Poor Dad. During the thing with Melinda, though, he did venture to say something — "Luke, you're young, boy. I wish I was your age again. Be happy, boy."

That's the cold, dark place. Whenever I'm confronted with something that makes me feel helpless, I feel the suction of this place, then scramble to escape it.

This is what I'm thinking when I see the parked red car ahead, with four white guys around it. A current shoots through me. It's too late to change direction, so I keep on toward them, eyes riveted to the sidewalk. I feel them watching, with their smirks, and all I can think is, "Get past them, past them."

They say people on high ledges have to struggle against looking down. As I pass just a couple of yards from them, my eyes dart to them for a split second. Crown is there, leering as he leans against the car. So is Toohey. So is that fat guy from gym who encouraged Toohey. So is Terry Monahan, a leather-jacketed kid with stringy hair, also in my history class.

I'm past them now.

"Move your black ass." Crown's voice.

I fight to keep from moving faster. Then I hear Toohey. "Fix your window yet?"

As my brain ignites, my one thought is, "Don't turn, don't turn and yell your guts out." They're laughing. Then I'm thinking, "Let them come after me, let them come and I'll go down ripping, tearing." I'm still walking. "Don't turn back."

All the way home the words are a bomb, a white flash going off with each pulse. A car brakes and honks me. Another corner, another street. Far off, my fingers are imbedded in the books at my hip. "Fix your window yet?"

At home, in my room, I sink onto the bed. My stomach is still a snake pit. And as I work at breathing evenly, the breaths rise and fall with five words I mutter: "They don't deserve to live."

In my sleep I scramble along, swiping at white faces and not hitting them. I swipe and claw and they're out of reach, smirking. "Fix your window yet?"

Mom's call for dinner wakes me.

Rhonda gets the phone call just after dinner. "Oh no!" She shudders, gripping the receiver with both hands. "Oh no. How . . ." Mom stands holding a plate. Dad looks up from his newspaper. I sit and stare.

"Rhonda, what is it?" Mom blurts.

Rhonda hangs up and steps into the kitchen. Her eyes gleam and she's still shaking. "Wilbur's in the hospital," she quavers. "He might die." I see her teeth come together as she turns away. Hurrying for the stairs, she screams: "Those pigs!"

Maybe it's only guys like Wilbur, and not guys like me, who get to be martyrs—partly because they naturally attract the fist and club, and partly because they crave being sculpted into the rock of Struggle. If that's so, it suits me okay. But I hope Wilbur pulls through.

September 30th

Nate details it for me on the bus; he heard it from his mother, who I guess knows Wilbur's mother. Wilbur has a concussion, a bad one. For a while they thought his skull was cracked. Several bones are broken. There was some internal bleeding. Whoever it was cornered him two blocks from the school.

"Coulda been me or you," Nate murmurs.

I look behind me and Rhonda's sitting alone, staring out the window.

In English, Mrs. Rollins's little smile twitches to life only once — as she explains the narrative device in a Henry James story—then fades. The book quivers in her hand. After the bell, I see her shuffling papers at her desk, and she has this washed-out appearance that makes her seem like an old woman or a child, pondering a broken toy or keepsake. Why does someone like her have to be here now?

Irwin drones, pauses, drones. This man's lungs and throat must be lined with years' worth of chalk dust. He never seems to look right at us. As he taps out another problem, I realize I'm lost and decide to make the most

45

of it by thinking about McBride's class, two periods away. Since getting dressed this morning, I've been trying to fortify myself, to hold a stoic attitude. I've held it while kids around me have whispered and muttered about Wilbur — about whether he'll die, about who might have done it and why. Still, I can only do this to a point. I know, for instance, how my insides will react when I eventually lay eyes on Crown or Toohey or the other two. Beyond that, there's McBride. What will he do?

I wonder about it again in the cramped quiet of the library. The teachers are pretty much as I would have guessed — Rollins with her quivering book, Irwin with the drone and ducking eyes, and now Hoffmann, white and straight as ever, walking among the tables. But how will McBride be now?

I'm watching a bony white boy, one of the last to come in, who's had to take a table with Law and his friends. The boy sits stiffly, holding a book. Law leans back, folds his arms, and stares across at the kid, who shifts position and turns a page. Law's friends also take long looks at the guy, making him feel it.

Jennie Davis files her nails at a corner table. She hasn't giggled or spoken at all yet. Beside me, Nate rests his head in his hands. Hoffmann stands watch at the counter. I wish it weren't this quiet.

When I walk into history, the first thing I see is Crown taking his seat, and the heat goes off inside me. Noticing me, he gives a minor sneer before looking away. I suppose I don't rate any more than that.

McBride enters as I sit and leans on his desk while the kids take their places. My mental prepping didn't do much good; watching him, I sink. He looks like he did on Monday—maybe worse—with the frown and eye-wrinkles.

"Okay," he says. "Today I'd like to move on to the next chapter."

My face is still hot from seeing Crown. And there's this bristling at the back of my head, which after a moment I realize is impatience, bordering on anger. It takes me another moment to realize the object. I'm impatient with McBride, and through the period I try to decipher the whys of it.

It's true that boredom has dropped on me like a curtain whenever Rhonda or Wilbur has spoken of injustice, racial oppression, rocks and windows and graffiti and Flower Heights and This Society and blah blah blah. And it's true that now, with bad dreams looming real, I've sort of lost my taste for "open discussion" of "vital issues." Talk—so often it seems so pointless.

But somehow I want to hear McBride say something about what has happened. I want to hear him speak from his mind and heart, to face the monster before our ignorant eyes and shove it back. I want him—just for now—to be a brown angel, to douse the smirks, loosen the fists, draw all this pain and mess into the warm, sane framework of his teaching. Tomorrow he can be a regular man again. For now, what I want from him is an overview, a good way of seeing everything, and from that, the will to hang tough.

I remember he verged on this yesterday with his talk about stages. Why didn't he pick that up again today, instead of the next chapter? With blood just shed, the time is riper than ever. Why didn't he say, "I want to speak to you about what happened to Wilbur"? We would

47

have sat silent and listened. Crown would have had to listen. Law would have. Nate needs it, like I do.

"In 1777," McBride is saying, "something besides the victory at Saratoga happened in America's favor. What was it?"

The answer is French aid, but I don't raise my hand. McBride's manner is hurried, distracted.

Then it hits me that maybe I'm sickeningly naive. Me and my expectations.

McBride stands before the desk where Wilbur sat yesterday, where Wilbur called history shit. He has at last gotten the answer he wanted. "Right, the French came into the war," he says. "And what American diplomat secured this help?"

No answer.

"Bob?"

A black guy wrinkles his brow.

"Sandy?"

A white girl looks apologetic. "I can't remember."

I'm bristling again. McBride's beginning to look as I thought he never would—misguided. This isn't his style. Does he really hope to force us back in time by peppering us with questions? On this day? You hear my thoughts, McBride?

"Come on, it's a big name," he says.

Well, shit. I figure Ben Franklin's a good guess, and am about to raise my hand when McBride points toward the back.

"Jennie?"

I look over my shoulder and Jennie's back there, chin resting on her forearms. Her big eyes look a bit glazed.

Since school started McBride has picked her out several times, and only about twice has she managed any kind of answer. It's like asking a wino to spot you a five, and the fact that he'd pick her out this morning strikes me as kind of . . . perverse.

"This is really easy," McBride urges, sounding annoyed.

Jennie leans back. I look ahead again, wanting to be out of here. Then Jennie's voice hits my ears: "Ohhh, Oscar, I really don't know."

Laughter leaps up through the class. I jerk my head around, and Jennie's got her chin on her forearms again; her expression is unchanged. The giggles trail off, but nearly everyone is looking at her with unsteady smiles. Not smiling, I look at McBride again. For a moment he's not smiling either. Oscar is his name, but until now it hasn't been a point of humor.

"Well, Jennie," he says, smiling a little. "Oscar's disappointed you didn't know it was Ben Franklin."

More laughter, less loud. Jennie yawns.

"Remember that, now," he almost mumbles. "Old Ben Franklin."

It happens on the way to lunch. Jennie is walking ahead of me, kind of sauntering along, but I'm too wrapped up with what she did to be admiring her ass. With what she did, and what McBridge didn't do. He seemed like just a teacher, one of the ordinary ones, afraid the floor would wobble and make him fall. Being so absorbed, I barely notice a short blond girl standing by a window, digging through her pocketbook . . . until Jennie, passing close, jumps on her. The girl shrieks. People leap back as Jennie, clutching the girl's hair, throws her against the wall.

Jennie grins like a lunatic. "I'm gonna tear your hair out, honeypie!"

The girl screams again as Jennie lunges. A white guy grabs Jennie and she kicks him, then hits him in the face, cursing. The blond girl cowers by the wall, crying. My arms twitch to life and I move to grab Jennie.

Suddenly Mrs. Hoffmann is there and seizes Jennie by the arms. Jennie trys to yank free—"Let go me, you white bitch!" Hoffmann's glasses drop to the floor, but her hold is firm.

Then Mrs. Jessup rushes up, her wide, dark face full of horror. She grabs Jennie from behind. Someone hands Hoffmann her glasses, and she and Jessup drag Jennie to the office. Jennie's curses fill the corridor as she squirms and pulls.

Shaking, the little blonde picks up her pocketbook as her friends surround her to see how she is. I move on.

It strikes me how strong the urge is to duck your head, to pass on by and dodge whatever involvement you can. A new bitterness enters me, a fresh hate. I see now, as maybe I should have seen yesterday in the locker room, that the curse is double-edged. Around here it's not just easy to get hurt. It's also awfully easy to be a coward. Excuses may follow—that inner dialogue about odds and complications—but they can't erase a naked failure, a failure that could occur at any moment, in any form, and maybe stain you for good.

And then another thought shoots in, so quickly that I

nearly stop walking. Could this be what McBride is feeling now?

Full of this question, I almost miss Rhonda as she passes me, carrying her books. Eyes blurred, face listless. She doesn't notice me.

I've just sat with my tray when I hear a voice: "Mind if I sit with you?"

I look up and it's Holly, holding her tray.

"No, have a seat," I say quickly.

And she sits. But I'd rather be alone. Nice as it might be, this little surprise could be the last straw for my digestion.

"You think Walker will have our reports ready today?" she asks.

"Doubt it." I open my milk carton. I don't mean to seem closed, but I really wish I were alone. A few seconds pass, and when I finally look at Holly, our eyes meet.

"You hear what just happened?" she asks.

"Yeah," I nod. "I was there."

"Sue Underwood nearly got her hair yanked out."

"It was bad," I say. "Jennie's crazy."

Holly picks at her food. She looks very good and seems about as nervous as I am, wanting to talk for some reason.

"How's it going for you?" I ask.

I guess my tone wasn't too subtle, since she looks away, then looks back and smiles. "Oh, better." She pauses. "My parents . . . they're getting divorced. It's kind of weird."

"Must be worse than weird sometimes."

She nods.

Bad luck is democratic. Often it even seems to lean toward nicer people. "Well," I say, "I know it'd be a real killer if it ever happened with my folks."

She shrugs. "My brother told me I should grow up about it, and he's probably right. I'll survive."

"Good." I know people must be looking at us.

"Actually I feel worse for my mother than for me."

Holly's trouble feels so far in nature from my own. At least most of mine isn't based right in my home. The idea of Mom and Dad doing the split—I can't picture what it would be like. Already I've run out of words. Not very helpful.

"Jennie was acting up in McBride's class too," I say. Real graceful transition.

Holly shakes her head. "Poor Mr. McBride."

There's something knowing in the remark, and I recall that she said her mother was on the school board.

"Holly, do you know much about McBride?"

She wipes her lips with her napkin. "Some," she says. "I had him for independent study last year, when he first came here. We connected really well. We still talk sometimes. I think he's pretty special." She pauses, then seems to sense that I want more. "He's taught in a bunch of places, I guess. He was in Louisville when busing started there. And New York. Cleveland too, I think. Inner-city places."

"Hard-core, huh?"

She nods with soft gravity. "Not the best places for a person."

"I know. I went to Randolph."

"Oh, you did?" She seems impressed. "Must have been fun. Anyway, he had a breakdown."

My hands drop to my lap and I stare at her. She looks back gravely, then stares down at her food, apparently sorry that she's caused me any shock.

"Really?" I say. "I mean, the guy seems so . . . like he's pretty solid."

"Oh, he is," she replies quickly. "People often come back stronger from something like that. In fact, that's just what he said to me about my case."

Once again my food has lost its appeal.

"After he got better he taught at some private school downstate," Holly goes on carefully. "Then he came here."

I nod.

"Does that upset you?" she asks.

"I'm just surprised. It's just that his class—it's the only one I like."

"Yeah," she mumbles. "He's a great one." She moves her fork around in her spinach; I don't think she's going to finish either. "Luke," she says, "I can't wait to get out of here."

I hadn't known you could be stung by gratitude, but I'm suddenly stung by it, toward this girl I hardly know. "Neither can I," I say. "But we'll get through."

A wry smile comes to her lips.

When lunch ends we walk to chemistry—getting some looks on the way—and sit together through the lecture, up front, helping to mark the black-white border down the middle. I'm surprised to feel a certain calm as I sit next to her, and it seems that in the simple talk at lunch we exchanged a trust. The faces around us fade. Walker's voice fades. And it's as though, through a glimmer of luck, we've found a quiet corner away from the heat. A foot of air separates my arm from hers, but it feels like less. It feels good.

The calm ends with the next bell. Reentering the swirl of the corridor, Holly and I say "See ya later" and head in opposite directions. As I turn I catch a burning look from Chuck Cameron. He was probably watching us all through class.

Hoffmann reads from the textbook, her Spanish inflections perfect. Two hours ago she grappled with crazy Jennie and had those glasses knocked from her face. Now she stands up there as calm as always, and as the class repeats her sentences, I think she scares me a little. But at the last bell she abruptly sits at her desk and starts reading some papers. I've never seen her do anything abruptly.

In the library, I read my English assignment and wait for the bus home.

When I get on the bus, Rhonda is there in her usual seat. Nate's further back, looking worn out, and doesn't seem to notice me. I sit beside Rhonda, but we say nothing on the way home. I don't believe she's looked at me once since yesterday. There are paint flecks on her hands; usually Rhonda spends any free time at school in the art room. The art teacher, Mrs. Sokoloski, considers her a prize talent.

When we arrive home, Nate's parents are visiting. Mom's sitting with them at the kitchen table and talking seriously over coffee. They go quiet as we enter the kitchen. Rhonda says hello and goes upstairs. Mr. Chisholm, a squat man with a gray mustache, nods hello to me and draws deeply on a cigarette. He seems worked up about something. Mrs. Chisholm is a plump lady with a worried smile.

I get a cup of coffee for myself and leave them, but stop in the living room to listen in.

"It's going to get worse, Beth," Mr. Chisholm tells Mom. "Once this petition gets around, we'll have a lot more on our hands than we bargained for."

"But Joe, are you sure about this?" Mom asks. "Where did you hear about it?"

"Heard it at work. That's why I came home early."

"Well, then, it's still just a rumor."

"Pretty damn *likely* rumor," Mr. Chisholm rumbles. "Judas, it make me wanna smash—"

"Joe, Joe—all right." Mrs. Chisholm speaks. "You make me scared for your heart."

"Humph! My heart," he grumbles.

"We've been real worried, Beth," Mrs. Chisholm says. "The white man next door's been harassing us."

"Goddamn bum," Mr. Chisholm fumes.

"And Nate's been telling us what it's like at school," Mrs. Chisholm adds. "We worry about him. And we worry about Lyle, our eldest. He's had trouble too. And it's so awful about the Shaw boy."

I take my coffee to my room.

Later I remember something I have to do, and I call

the police department. I'm put on hold, and it's a few minutes before a sergeant comes on and I tell him about Toohey's little question. I also mention the shower incident with Wilbur, and point out that Toohey and the others were around when Wilbur was beaten. He says they'll check up on it and I thank him.

Though I'm not eager for details about the petition story, I'm a good guesser, and it turns out to be what I thought. After dinner I'm watching the news with Mom and Dad when she eases into the subject. At dinner I wondered whether she'd tell us at all, feeling her tussle with it between questions about Dad's day.

Mr. Chisholm said that some white residents are circulating a petition, more or less on the sly, to block further black movement into Flower Heights. Apparently the Chisholms also think that some murkier plans are shaping to pressure black residents into leaving.

I pretend to watch TV but can't help glancing at Dad as he listens. My father's not a volatile guy like Mr. Chisholm, but in his face I see a hint of the same caged look.

He waits a moment, then shrugs. "We'll see, I guess."

Upstairs I bury myself in homework, but I keep thinking of what Holly told me about McBride.

October 1st

Mrs. Rollins gives us a pitifully easy test this morning, based on characters in the stories we've read. I finish it fast and spend the rest of the period watching her freckled hands fidget with a paperweight—a white stone with a little red rose painted on it.

Jennie has been suspended for the rest of the week; I regret it wasn't for longer. The word is that she swallowed something potent yesterday morning.

I don't look forward to gym period. The locker room's quieter than usual, and this gets to Lattanzio. "Come on, you're moving like old ladies!" he urges as we dress. Tying my sneakers, I see Toohey pass by in his underwear. He doesn't see me. A pause for evaluation—he's a couple of inches shorter than I, limber and baby-faced. If he'd just look at me once, I'd give him a good stare, a stare straight into his ape brain. I think of the window and how it would be great to kick him in the balls. Walking into the gym, I think of the window and how it would be great to hit him in the stomach, then the face.

An all-black game begins under the far-end backboard. Accompanied by his fat friend, Toohey joins a larger, all-white game at the other end. "Hey, lemme get a shot!" he yells. Let me get a shot at you, prick.

Holding a ball, I stand to the side and watch him. The flash goes off in me again and I'm going to do it. When we head for the showers, I'll punch him, hard enough to make him puke. And I don't care what happens. I feel crazy. Let them get me if they want.

Barry McLeod is beside me. "You wanna go one-on-one?" he asks.

"Sure," I say, and give him the ball. "You take it out first."

I don't play as I usually do. I play hard, grimly, making steals under the net, shooting and rebounding better than I have before.

Barry is a nice guy. He apologizes when we bump, praises me on a long basket. I beat him 20–14.

When Lattanzio's whistle shrieks, we walk back, talking a little about Spanish, and as I cool off I realize I'm not going to smash Toohey. The fire has left my brain. Besides that, the sudden thought of Wilbur makes my mood more practical.

Barry asks how I like Flower Heights; I say I think I'm getting used to it, and how long has he lived here? Most of his life, he says, on Cedar Drive, a few blocks from the school.

The fire returns, just a bit, when Toohey passes my bench on the way to the showers. For a second he sees me. He sees my eyes. And my eyes say this: "Wanna shove another nigger?"

And he strides on past. God, to kick him in the balls.

*   *   *

Today I'm not trying to will any great acts from McBride. Instead, as I watch him I'm imagining an invisible fissure down his middle, the crack of his past.

"Okay, folks," he begins.

No inward pleading from me today; if things go passably well, that will be fine. But I can't deny that the American Revolution, with its Franklins and Saratogas, has lost its taste.

"What happened," he asks, "when Washington attacked at Monmouth?"

I raise my hand. "General Lee led the attack, then retreated as soon as the fighting started."

"Right," he says. "And Washington supposedly cursed him till the leaves shook. So after a drawn battle, the British made it to New York." He clears his throat and takes a breath. "Now around this time the Americans had begun to get help from foreign military men who were very valuable. Can anyone name some of these?"

It's a policy of mine not to answer two questions in a row. Bookworms get snickered at, and I hate snickers. It's also one of the reasons that, as an English teacher at Randolph once pointed out, I often talk differently from the way I think. But as the quiet stretches, I find my hand up again.

"Yes, Luke?"

"Lafayette, Von Steuben, DeKalb."

"Very good," McBride says as two white girls trade mock-impressed glances. Stupid bitches. And McBride asks on: "And how were these men so useful?"

What's with all these questions? He didn't used to ask so many.

Silence. Sorry, McBride.

61

"Terry?" He points to Monahan, who sits next to Crown. Like Crown, he's slouched in his chair.

For a long moment he sits there with a toothy smile. McBride waits. Then, slowly, the kid's shoulders rise in a shrug. A very blank, very practiced shrug. Jennie couldn't have done better. And there's a ripple of laughter through the room.

Unsmiling, McBride stares at him. "If you don't know, use your tongue, okay?"

The quiet falls again. Then McBride runs through the august accomplishments of Lafayette, Von Steuben, and DeKalb, bless 'em.

Minutes later the room empties, and as I stand I catch a look from McBride. At least I think it's for me. A look starker than my father's, or Holly's, or Nate's, that strikes me still. A glum, tired glance. And suddenly my wrappings of patience are gone, torn away. No matter what he's had to endure, that was never the kind of glance I wanted from Oscar McBride.

Just then there's a shout from the crowded doorway, followed by a doglike swirl of shoving and curses as kids jump aside.

"Motherfuck!" Law spits, pushing Crown off.

"Fucking bastard!" Crown hisses, hunching with fists forward. "I'll fucking kill—"

McBride, who has whirled around, takes two quick strides toward them and stops short. "Stop it! Back off!" he sputters, arms raised. "George, get back!"

Crown snarls at Law. "Keep your black ass outa my way!"

"I'll kick your head in, you—"

"All right, shut up!" McBride yells. But his yell is almost a screech, more frantic plea than command. And he stands there, not quite between them, fingers trembling at his sides as everyone watches.

"All right," he breathes. "Both of you sit down—"

"What's going on?" a voice demands. Principal O'Donnell, tall and white-haired, appears in the doorway and fires a look at Law and Crown. "Come with me!" he snaps, grabbing each by the arm. They head for the office. McBride follows.

The other kids leave quickly. Nate gives me a backward glance as he goes out. After standing in the cleared room for a minute, I leave too, having felt something move beneath my feet.

This time I find Holly sitting alone in the cafeteria and sit with her.

"Eating alone must be contagious," I say.

"Well, I'm just sick of my usual company," she says. "I realized it last week. Party talk, boyfriend talk . . ."

Lunch is lousy. As I try to make headway with it I feel her eyeing me.

"Something the matter?" she asks.

And I tell her about Law and Crown's latest bit of friction. She shakes her head. "We'd all be better off if they got expelled."

"We'd be better off if they killed each other!" I blurt. She stops eating, and I see I've shocked her.

"I didn't really mean that," I say. "It's just that . . ."

"I know," she says.

I turn my fork over in my fingers. Then I chuckle. "A few days ago a friend of mine said something like that and I looked at him like you just looked at me."

"Bad thoughts come easy," she says. And she pats my hand. "I know that better than anybody. Let's change the subject."

"You read my mind," I say, and proceed to tell her about Rollins's joke test. But my mind keeps churning up the scene in McBride's class — the curses, the near-screech, his trembling fingers. There are people who can block things out — Hoffmann, maybe, for one — and I wish I were one of them. During my last big-league depression, when that girl Melinda was icing me back at Randolph, I dug out a book on psychology just to see how I'd be classified. What was it I read about the obsessive personality? Fine word, "obsessive." I think there was also a chapter on nervous breakdowns.

But now Holly's telling me about a trip she and her mother wil be taking this weekend, up to the Huron Hills to see the foliage. I don't really listen, I just watch her blue eyes dance, the smooth lines of her face. I'm surprised at how suddenly I've come to this feeling about her. When she smiles, a bit of euphoria twirls up in me, the surroundings fade, and we're in that quiet corner. A warmth comes over me when I think of how someone like her would pick me over others to talk to. That's how it felt nearly a year ago at Randolph, with a girl named Joanne. She was as pretty as Holly, though dreamier. Joanne had a nice voice and wanted to be a singer. We went out a few times and were just getting heavy when her family had to move out west. There was really no one before, and there's been nobody since.

"It'll be good for you and your mom to get away and talk about things." I say.

"It was my idea." She nods. "It's a way of letting her know she still has me to have fun with. That even though Dad's gone . . . You want my carrot cake?"

"No, thanks."

Her eyes aren't dancing. "I don't want to burden you with all this stuff."

"Burden me."

She laughs, then chews her cake. The way she looks at me has changed; it's more delicate, almost timid. "You know, I hated both of them off and on. My brother— he's older—he practically took it in stride. For a while I just froze up whenever my father came around. Then, the last time, he took me to a restaurant and sat there with a drink, going on about his law practice. And I started to feel sorry for him . . ."

As Holly talks I happen to see Cameron pointing out the two of us from a table where he's sitting with a bunch of other kids. They look. I look away, and my gaze falls on Holly's white neck. The euphoria leaves.

Sitting with her in chemistry, I don't need to glance at Cameron to feel his glower, and to feel in myself a hate I can't think down. Crown, Toohey, and now Cameron. Within a few days I've become a collector of hates. Or are they collecting me?

The touch of Holly's hand felt nice. And it dawns on me that facts are facts. If we get any more obvious than we have, publicly, I might as well hit Toohey in gym and let the furnace suck me in.

*   *   *

The library is sanctuary again as I work on my lab report and wait for the bus. Mrs. Wells busily stamps books at the counter. Then Mrs. Rollins enters with a stack of papers. She notices me, smiles like a pixie, and comes over with one of the papers.

"Luke," she says in her confiding way, "your test was beautiful." I look and see I aced it. "Thanks," I say, for lack of anything else. "I wasn't sure I got the one on Henry James."

"Well, you got it," she notes brightly. Her fluttery air is more distinct than usual; her china-blues are blinking, almost in a twitch. And I feel she wants to talk more. "You're a fine student," she adds.

"Thank you," I say.

"It's just such a shame . . ." Her eyes fall in the little-girl manner. "It's such a shame that good students like you have to go through all that's been happening."

Yes ma'am, I think, I could do without it. "It can't be easy for you either," I say.

"Oh, it isn't, Luke." She blinks—so earnest. "When I see kids here getting so hostile . . ." She wipes a blond strand from her forehead. "I just want to hide."

I'm not beyond pity yet, because I feel it for her now, once again. I have to come up with a response.

"Maybe it'll be okay by Christmas," I offer. "You know, tempers go down with the temperature."

"Oh, I hope so, Luke. Everything's happening so fast." She doesn't leave me but gazes out the window. "My husband and I used to teach at a small school in the country. Sometimes I wish I were back there."

"I don't blame you," I say.

She's quiet for a moment, sighs, then looks at my open

66

chemistry book. She brightens. "Well, I'll let you work. But listen, take care of yourself."

I can tell she's completely sincere. What a nice lady. "We'll get through," I say with a smile—that all-purpose phrase.

"Yes, we will." She sighs. "You know, there's just no reason why black people and white people can't be friends. There's just no reason."

What a nice, pathetic lady.

"See you tomorrow, Luke."

"Okay. Thanks, Mrs. Rollins." And she goes to her table to correct more tests.

After a minute I gather my books and walk to the side doors. Rhonda's there, leaning back against a radiator. Outside, the fall-fired leaves rustle, and clouds move overhead in the pale sunlight. The Stars and Stripes flaps on its pole.

I'm staring out absently when two figures appear from around a far corner of the building and head down the path toward the street. One stops to rub a cigarette into the ground—he's Ray Powers, a thickset friend of Law's. The other one is Nate. As they reach the sidewalk, a dented, paint-blotched car pulls up, and they get in before it drives away.

When the bus comes I sit with Rhonda. It strikes me that I've hardly heard her speak since Tuesday night, and an urge hits to ask her something, to prod a few words from her. But as I watch that face, that lovely, royal face staring out with eyes that have fallen on me so often like a withering ray, a bitter taste rises. I'm not going to be the one to talk. Why'd I even sit with her?

Home. My parents are stepping gingerly this evening,

around us and around each other. Mom especially. At the dinner table she says that she has heard nothing more of the petition, but she has trouble supplying the usual talk. To help her out I mention my English test, which pleases the two of them.

Then Mom asks Rhonda if she's heard anything about Wilbur's condition. Rhonda says she called the hospital and he's stable. She says that she and some others presented a letter with a bunch of signatures to Principal O'Donnell. She wrote the letter, which demanded that the school take steps to increase the safety of black students. O'Donnell said he was as concerned as they were, that measures would be taken, and then he left for a meeting.

"Huh," Dad says, eating his ham. "Real specific. The man oughta run for Congress."

Afterward, while I'm doing the dishes, Dad can't find the newspaper. "How come it gets lost so easy around here?" he demands. Right away Mom hunts it up, and he takes it with an awkward thank-you.

Like any couple, Mom and Dad argue once in a while, usually over minor stuff like a phone bill or a news item. As exasperated as they may sound, there's always an undercurrent of fun, as if beneath their voices they're laughing at themselves. They seem younger, more alive. "Fred, will you listen?" "Beth, if I listened to you they'd have to put me in a mental hospital." "The way you talk, you belong in one already." "Great, maybe in there I'd find somebody who made more sense than you." Tonight I'd welcome the sound of an argument like that.

October 2nd

Nate is especially talkative at the bus stop.

"I just wish George had got his chance at Crown," he's saying. "He woulda killed him this time. I mean it, man. It's gonna happen."

I feel kind of self-conscious because a few of the white kids are staring at Nate. He notices and lowers his voice. Rhonda's sitting on the grass at the curb, not listening.

Then Nate speaks to her. "You hear anything about Wilbur?"

She nods. "They operated Wednesday. Looks like he'll make it." Her voice is unusally soft.

The bus comes, and when Nate sits with me, I tell him I saw his folks Wednesday—nice people. But quickly he steers me back to the subject of Crown's impending death—"him and that whole bunch of white shits he hangs out with."

His voice isn't low enough for my taste; I turn to see who's looking. What I see is Rhonda, staring not out the window this time but into her lap. On her smooth brow are the faintest lines, and I can see her breathing, the barely detectable rise and fall of her shoulders. I can't take my eyes away. Her bottom lip quivers.

Nate is tapping my arm and I turn to him. "What?"

"I'm saying, if things get any worse we're gonna have to stick together." Nate makes a thin fist, his face intent.

"Yeah, could be," I say.

When I look back at Rhonda again, she has resumed her regular bus-ride pose.

The stops are made. We arrive. We scatter for homeroom.

"Niggers Go Home."

The words, scrawled on the blackboard, greet us in Irwin's room. People look at each other as they sit, and no one says anything. In the corner of my eye, that center aisle — black side, white side — seems wider, and if someone dared to stick a hand into that space, I feel, it might crackle like a force field from "Star Trek." Irwin's hurried entrance is a relief; relief has some odd sources these days. He doesn't notice the board until he's seated behind his desk. Then he jumps up, grabs an eraser, and wipes the board clean with quick, robotic strokes. As he does I hear him mutter something. Seated again, he starts taking attendance.

"Here," each voice answers.

"Luke Parrish."

"Here." Here again, and I can't even thank that rascally God it's Friday.

In English, Mrs. Rollins's animation is more pronounced this morning, her speech faster, which makes me think that she's finally acquired that aversion to in-between silences. When she finishes reading a passage from the story we're on, she doesn't let the book quiver but holds it firmly to her chest—a subtle change in style for which I'm thankful. At the bell, fatigue crosses her face like a cloud, as though she has just sprinted her roundish body down a long road.

Irwin gets annoyed next period when he can't get the correct answer to a problem out of us. Shaking his head, the little man pivots to the board and taps out the answer —*tap, t-tap, tap.* For all this, he's acting more distracted than usual, looking outside more often than we do.

Then comes the enforced silence of the library, and Hoffmann's phantomlike passing among the tables. One little item—Nate's at Law's table, knuckles resting on his unopened book. Now and then he whispers with Law or Ray Powers. As my eyes wander around the room, I wonder what shift of ground will occur when McBride faces us again.

When I get to history, Law and Crown are in their usual places, on opposite flanks, and in their usual postures. Each is talking to kids seated attentively around him.

McBride stands at his desk, thumbing through the corrected tests. He looks tired.

One of the first things I notice is that half the class is sitting extra low in their seats, seemingly prepared for boredom, or maybe saving strength for straightening up if a new skirmish occurs. *That* won't be boring, will it? Or maybe they think boredom looks good on Law and Crown. I find I'm sitting that way too, arms draped across my desktop. Prepared for boredom, saving strength. Nate's into the pose also—strange for a kid who was so wired on the bus—but on him it looks like an amateur version of Wilbur. Wilbur was the champ, all right. His empty desk is a kind of monument up front.

Nate chews his thumbnail—bad technique.

"I'm sorry to say the tests were pretty disappointing for the most part," McBride says. "There were six flunks. I haven't decided whether I'll give make-ups for it, but we'll go over it after I pass these back."

He passes them back, moving down one aisle and up the next, and there's only the sound of paper. I avoid his face, not wanting to see the strain, that thin fissure. Let him look that way, I think. Again I'll be content with a holding action—as long as it works this time. Gather what you have, McBride, and keep your eye on Law and Crown.

My desires in this classroom have shrunk with each day's erosion of order. Small is *not* beautiful.

His hand lays the test before me—a 97, an A. I glance over at Nate's paper—67, a D-plus—but not at his face.

The period is taken up with going over the test. I doze along. Then McBride's voice rises: "You listening, George?"

I look back and Law is talking to the girl across from him.

"George?" McBride repeats.

Law looks up. "What's that, Oscar?"

The flurry of giggles. I look out the window. This time I don't care to keep my ears open. But, staring off, I listen anyway, picturing how McBride must be—grim-faced, I hope, not startled.

"To me you're George," he says after a pause. "To you I'm Mr. McBride. You hear me, George?"

I can't help looking, so I do. McBride stands much as I'd pictured him, straight and staring. But his expression —I wish it were harder, less sad. That's how he looks with those wrinkled eyes—more sad than angry, more tired than commanding. Nate's expression is interesting; he seems transfixed, caught between anxiety and expectancy. I don't look at Law.

"I said, do you hear me?" McBride repeats. By themselves his words are fine; if only they were all that counted.

"Yeah," Law mumbles.

Another silent space—good. McBride seems to have won the skirmish. As the dust of this exchange settles around him, so does a residue of strength.

"Then there's the second essay question," he resumes. "It asked for a list of causes for the conflict, but a lot of you didn't specify the acts of parliament that—"

"Os-*cuh!*"

Twisted laughter, louder than before. The voice came from the white side, and when I shoot a glance through the giggling faces, Terry Monahan is leaning forward over his desktop, hands cupped to his mouth. McBride is looking but clearly doesn't spot him.

The laughs end as quickly as they started, and McBride looks again at his test copy. "As I was saying . . ." he goes on.

Doesn't he see what's happening? What's *been* happening? His face tells me he does, so why doesn't he turn to thunder?

When class ends, I get out fast. As I snatch up my book, however, I see McBride signal Law to step over.

And going through the doorway, I look back (my neck has a will of its own, it seems), and the two are standing a foot apart, McBride talking in a low tone. Law stands broad-chested and a little taller, one thick arm dangling, the other hand on his hip. A few black guys remain seated, watching. Nate is one of them.

In the cafeteria, I scan for Holly, eager to sit. There's no sign of her, so I go to an empty corner table.

It's good to be alone, I think, cutting a meatball. Good to feel obscure, here on the periphery of the voice-rumble and the clinking of forks on plates, though it would be nicer with Holly. And as for McBride's class, my mind has disengaged. It's not hammering me. Maybe detachment is an acquired skill.

By chance I spot Holly, way on the other side with a bunch of her friends. Her back is to me and a girl is talking to her. Cameron is beside the other girl, watching them as he eats.

So they beat me to her today.

When I next look up, I realize that I have the whole panorama before me. Over there, Law joins his buddies at their usual table. Between mouthfuls they throw hot-eyed, vaguely expectant glances about them, talking through smirks. Same as always, only more so.

Up there are Crown and his bunch, including Toohey and Monahan. Hunched and leering, a little louder than Law's table.

And there, over in the corner, is Rhonda. She and the people I saw her and Wilbur with before. She's seated on the end, eating slowly and not really looking at them as they converse in their serious manner. But they seem more subdued. They don't look complete, with their core gone. Wilbur was their core.

I see Nate coming down one aisle with his tray. He sits at one end of Law's table and spills his milk. Righting the carton quickly, he fixes his stare on Law, who's talking.

I take a draw on my milk straw and as I do, Irwin's voice enters my ear: "I don't know how it rates next to other schools, but jeez!" Looking to my left, I realize I'm two empty tables from where the teachers eat, and there's McBride talking with Irwin.

"I keep waiting for a real disciplinary crackdown, don't you?" Irwin's saying. "I mean a real one. It's getting to that point."

McBride's reply is too low to hear.

"Well, sure, sure," says Irwin. "There's always a price tag, but when the ship's sinking . . ."

McBride speaks, again too low.

Irwin nods, chewing his food. "Right, yeah." Then he shakes his head. "I'm telling you, Oscar"—he raises his free hand, fingers spread—"I'm proequality all the way, believe me. But when I heard about the ruling, I *knew* what was coming."

"So did I," McBride says, quite distinctly.

I stop listening, feeling the world of newsy terms yawn wide. Terms like "busing" and "integration." That second one especially. That abstraction, so easily spoken, that yields this heat, this ache; these eyes, these faces. This noise and silence, all around. Sputtered words. Bruises and blood. Yeah, terms are easy.

It's impossible for me to feel at the center of an issue

so easily named, though I know I am. I do feel at the center of something, all this that I see and sense, but it would be a joke to try to name it.

Mrs. Rollins would surely appreciate the irony—how my family moved out here the very summer a judge decided that *Brown* v. *Topeka* wasn't being properly observed, especially in the suburbs. Out here to green lawns and white neighbors, away from Douglas Street in the city, where paint peeled as the crime rate rose. We were still back there two months ago—it's strange, ridiculous, that it's been that short a time. A week before we moved, Dad witnessed a holdup at a hardware store the next block over. Then *flash,* and we were here, among whites, feeling hit from two sides. That judge, I heard on the news, has received several threats on his life.

I think about the bus-in kids. At least they return each day to homes with windows that, however dirty, won't get smashed by any rock from a white hand.

On the way to chemistry I pass Barry. Walking stiff-shouldered, he almost doesn't see me.

"Hi, Barry," I say.

"Hullo, Luke," he says, and we both keep on.

It's then that I realize I'm walking stiff-shouldered too. It would be good to know a guy like Barry a little better.

When I get to class, Cameron is seated beside Holly, at the desk where I sat the last couple of days. It must mean a lot to him, as it places him on the black side. So I sit near the door, and as Walker wields his pointer around the element chart, I send imaginary missiles into the back of Cameron's curly head.

At the bell, Holly stops me with a smile as I rise. "Thank God for Friday, huh?"

"Amen," I say, avoiding Cameron's face as he exits behind her. "You all set to head for the hills?"

"You bet. I may burn my books and stay there."

We walk into the hall. "I wish I was going someplace," I say.

"If I had the Subaru I want, I'd pick you up and take us to Mexico." She says this with a kind of forced lightness.

"I'd be willing to walk," I say. "Well, have a good time."

"Thanks. Have a good weekend," she replies, and as she turns I see her smile drop away.

I don't really wonder about it till after dictation in Spanish. The thing I felt while sitting with her yesterday, that dizzy dread—does she feel it too? Has she felt the glowers, the throb of unspoken law? And has she considered, as I have, that liking someone might be stupid?

Mom told me once about a cousin of hers who had a white girlfriend for a very short time. He was left for dead, with his head beaten in. The fact that that happened nearly two decades ago holds little comfort. Especially now that my feelings toward Holly seem to have their own momentum. Until recently I was dreaming a lot about Joanne, my friend who moved west. About being body-locked with her in the back seat of Dad's car, or some better setting. Now Holly has replaced Joanne in the fantasy. Only as soon as it starts running, my mind jerks back from it like fingers from a thornbush, and I'm there telling myself, "For Jesus' sake, I haven't even kissed her."

Hoffmann's white hand takes my paper. At this moment it hits me—I have to talk to McBride.

"Hello, Luke." He looks up from what he's writing. "How are you?"

"All right." I pull up a desk.

"Something you want to talk about?"

"Yeah."

I should have thought of a lead-off before coming in here—some light preamble. I didn't, and the vacant room seems to vibrate with a leftover force. A week has gone. I haven't spoken yet, and my stomach is tight.

"Is it about the test?" he asks. "Yours was one of the few bright spots."

I stare at his blotter. Goddamn it, you know it's not about the test.

"Okay," he says, very low.

He gets up, goes to the door and shuts it, then comes back, "It's about . . . the way things have been," he says, letting out a long breath.

"Yeah," I say. "It's about that."

He nods, and I open my mouth. "I've watched you," I manage.

"I know."

"I've seen what you've been going through."

McBride isn't looking at me; his eyes are lost among the empty rows. His gray sideburns look like spots where he's been singed. Then I see his jaw tighten. "It's part of being a teacher," he says flatly.

"I guess it is," I agree flatly.

"I'm sure it's hard times for you too," he says, looking at me now.

I don't comment.

"So what is it?" he asks.

"I've seen you up there, and I feel bad. I want to do something."

His fingers entwine on the blotter, and again his eyes move along the desks. "Or, more accurately, you want *me* to do something."

Sitting very still, I ask myself whether I have any right to do this. "You've done things," I say.

"Something more, then."

Now I can't look at him.

"I think about it, Luke," he says. "I was thinking about it when you came in. I'll be thinking after you leave."

I nod at his desk.

"I think about George and Andy," he goes on. "I also think about you."

I look at him, and behind the dark eyes I catch the intricate clicking of his intellect, all the learning in there like precious stones, disturbed now by something alien. A shadow crosses his face, and I just barely see him shiver.

"I think about you, and all the other kids who aren't really part of the trouble. But listen, I *know* I can't keep just thinking, I *know* I have to do something." One hand is clenched on the blotter. Again he shivers.

And I shiver too, because even as he speaks I see it again—the thin crack running down through him. How deep does it go? And how deep does mine go? I realize at once that the flaw I perceive in him, the thing that makes him tremble when hate mounts, mirrors and enlarges my own. For some time now I've had my own fissure, which widens when the cold tides hit, letting my will for life run out, the leaden feeling run in. It moves through my dreams, and I've cursed it while lying in the dark. But at least I still have my family as a small bastion at day's end. McBride's a grown man. The world expects him—as it will soon expect me—to meet the tides alone and remain standing. Despite anything, and despite whatever came before. What did come before?

His hand unclenches and he looks at the blotter. "Just . . . remember that," he mutters. He's embarrassed, and I should leave.

"Thank you," I say, and get up.

I stop at the door, my hand on the knob. "See you Monday, Mr. McBride."

Without looking up he makes an old man's smile, weary. "You know, I guess after a while we all get to be part of the trouble."

I turn the knob. "Yeah, I know. Thanks."

"See you Monday."

Headed down the hall, I think of his voice—the hushed declaration, verging on a plea.

The last time I spoke with him after school was three weeks back, when I was coming to think of him as pretty unique. We sat there talking about history for half an hour, like sharers of a happy secret.

Rhonda isn't on the return bus (Nate either), and as the streets wind by I start to worry a little. When I come in the door, I ask Mom if Rhonda's home and she says no.

In the living room, I put a record on low and sit for a while. Just before the record ends I hear the door open, then Mom's voice.

"I'm glad you're home. Luke said you weren't on the bus."

"A few of us took a car in to the hospital," Rhonda says, sounding tired.

"How is he?"

"They said he was sleeping."

Rhonda passes through the room and goes upstairs.

Dinner is more relaxed tonight than it's been all week, with the realization that Friday is still Friday. Dad's more talkative, though Rhonda's still quiet. So let her be, I think.

"We're out there on Western Boulevard," Dad says, "putting in flagstones. Then this Lincoln pulls up and a man jumps out hollering to beat hell. Some guy on the city council, it turned out. Anyway, seems his wife ordered the job and he canceled it, but somebody misplaced his message at the office." Dad laughs.

"I'm glad you're laughing about it, Fred," Mom says.

"Didn't mean trouble for me," he shrugs. "They said head on out to this address and do this, and no one was home, so I set them at it." He shakes his head, chuckling. "That guy, he was so mad."

I finish eating first and go to turn on the local news. A report comes on about racial problems in the city proper, but with a secondary focus on Flower Heights. I turn the sound low, glad that the others are still in the kitchen. The well-groomed white reporter is good with the serious tone: "Both white and black residents here are greatly concerned over the recent tension, new to this pleasant, growing community. The worry has been intensified by violence at Bently High School.'' Principal O'Donnell's chunky, dignified face fills the screen. "Certainly there's been distress among teachers and students at our school," he says. "But we're doing our utmost to root out the trouble. Strict action is being taken against those students perpetrating violence upon others, regardless of race.''

Mom and Dad come in for the network news. The President is defending his plan to sell more sophisticated arms to Saudi Arabia. Israelis demonstrate in front of the U.S. embassy in Tel Aviv. There's been a great flood of the Ganges River in India and 10,000 people are thought to be dead, with ten times that number homeless. A report examines the effects of cuts in college funding, and this touches off a debate between Mom and Dad.

"Of all the things to get cut!" Mom says. "Couldn't the Pentagon have done without a few missiles?"

"Yeah, maybe," Dad says. "But when times get like they've got, things like that give way.''

My father sweated his way out of Baltimore when he was a teenager, sweated through the Army and then through night school to earn an associate's degree. Sweat, though he talks little about it, was how he ever got anywhere, including here. To some extent I think I still romanticize his past, imagining that he overcame all those barriers by quiet pluck and muscle, through years that, God knows, were more heroic than my own.

"But Fred," Mom says, motioning to the set. "They don't seem to be bending over backwards to save that funding.''

"Maybe people will stop taking college for granted now," Dad replies. "Used to be a big, special thing thirty years back."

"Luke won't take it for granted, and neither will Rhonda." Mom motions at me, indignant. "What about them?"

Reminded of my presence, Dad looks at me and flickers a smile. "Oh, they'll get in and do fine, government or no."

"I'm glad you're confident." Mom sighs.

They argue and I can't hear the news, but I don't care. The house feels safe again.

Their exchange stops when a report about Ku Klux Klan activity comes on. We watch a line of white-hooded Klansmen marching past City Hall in Louisville. A squint-eyed grand dragon delivers a speech while onlookers jeer. "The Klan is picking up support from white Christian Americans everywhere!" he booms. "Because they know we represent their best interests! They know the problems of this country will be unsolved until the elements that are dragging it down are eradicated!"

Mom closes her eyes and seems to doze. Dad stares at the set, his lips tight.

"Wow," I say. "He knows how to say 'eradicated.' "

Neither remarks on my remark. The reporter, who is black, goes on to tell about the Klan's recruiting efforts nationwide, including high schools.

Rhonda comes down carrying her coat and handbag and catches the last shot—a night rally in Georgia, complete with flaming cross. The news ends.

"Where are you going?" Mom asks Rhonda.

"Over to visit Wilbur's parents," she says. "I feel I should."

"Rhonda, I don't know," Mom says, looking at Dad.

"You'd better not," Dad says.

"Why?" Rhonda asks. "It's only three blocks."

"It's a bad idea for a girl to be out walking at night," Dad says, shaking his head. "Especially now."

"Okay," says Rhonda. "Then could you drive me and pick me up later?"

He sighs. "Babe, I'm kind of tired. Listen, you can just call them."

"I want to see them. Let *me* have the car, then."

"You've only got your permit," Mom says. "Somebody has to be with you."

I'm about to offer to drive her, but then I look at Dad and decide not to.

"Anyway," Dad says with a wave of his hand, "I'd rather not have you go anywhere tonight."

"Daddy, their son's in the hospital!" Rhonda shouts. "They're still not sure how bad he is! I want to see if I can be of any help."

"Fine, but you can see them some other time," Dad tells her, his voice rising.

"I can go with you tomorrow," Mom offers.

"Wilbur's *my* friend!" Rhonda blurts, eyes glistening. "He's *my* business, and I just want to see what I can do!"

"Stop yelling," Mom tells her.

"You're staying in, Rhonda," says Dad.

She throws her coat and handbag in a chair. "That's right!" she shouts. "Make me hide inside the house like you! All you know how to do is hide!"

Dad gets to his feet, glowering. "Don't you get high and mighty, girl! If you had any sense you'd see—"

"*I'd* see?" she asks. "You mean *you* see what's going on? Do you need a burning cross on your lawn before you know we can't just hide?"

The vein in Dad's temple throbs, and for a moment his mouth is open but no sound comes out. Then he flares. "You think you need to tell me about it? You think you know so much? Well, let me tell you—"

Rhonda rushes to the stairs, and she's gone.

Dad drops onto the couch, his face smoldering, and Mom pats his arm. "It's really affecting her," she says.

"I know, I know," he grumbles. "I just wish . . ." He stops and makes a spitting sound. It's been years since I've seen him get that mad. Not since I punched the hole in my bedroom wall.

Rhonda spends the evening upstairs. Mom and Dad and I watch a long movie about British explorers in East Africa.

October 3rd–4th

The rock comes through the window, bouncing with broken glass off the kitchen table. From outside there's laughter. I look behind me, and Mom stands there with her hands to her mouth. "We're going back," she says, her voice shaking. "We can't live here."

I ask where Dad is.

"He's gone to sell the house," she says.

And I hear the laughter, a deep gurgling. Through the shattered pane I see them on the sidewalk — Crown, Toohey, Monahan, the fat one, and a few others, all laughter and leers.

I reach for the door and I'm outside, walking toward them, hunched, my throat contorted with curses I can't understand. Smiling, they watch me come, and then Crown is holding a knife by his hip.

Suddenly I'm in front of the school, standing before them. The sky is gray. Crown holds the knife. Then I see Law with a knife, over on the grass, surrounded by his bunch. Nate is with them, looking eagerly from Law to Crown.

Then McBride is coming across the grass, from the

direction of the building. He passes between the two groups and pushes me away. "Back off," he says. "I know I have to do something."

I back away and watch him there in the middle, caught between the leers. He stretches a hand each way, unsteadily, looking from Law's group to Crown's, then to Law's again. Then his brow wrinkles, his lips draw back, and his face is fear.

"Stop it!" he shrieks.

And they're closing on him—Law's group from their side, Crown's from theirs, closing around him with slow, easy, hulking movements.

"No! Stop!" McBride cries.

I can't move, can't yell, and he vanishes into the knot of light and dark skins, the smirking faces and dangling arms. Then there's no sound. The two gangs stand still, locked as one, then slowly separate. McBride lies on the ground between them, unmoving.

I turn and try to run but can only stagger. I fall on the grass, get up, make it to a corner of the building, near the driveway. Then I see two people walking up the driveway, away from me—Holly and Cameron. I call Holly's name, but she doesn't hear.

Then I feel a presence behind me and look to see Rhonda and Wilbur, side by side, with faces of stone. Wilbur's head is wrapped in a bloody bandage. I look at them, unable to speak.

"Go on," Rhonda speaks. "Run and hide."

I turn, stagger, and fall.

Then I wake up.

Set free in sleep, my subconscious often serves up evil

brew. All this past week I've awoken with vague images tussling in my head, the ripple of dreams which I then forget in the hurry for school. But this morning I have more than enough time to lie in bed, letting all the pictures settle and come clear.

As I do, I see the rock over on my bureau, and when I finally rise I walk over and pick it up. Each night it has watched me in the dark as I sleep. Now the mica eyes glint up, and the whole sensation of last Sunday rushes back. I squeeze the rock till my fist quivers. Then I want to throw it down, break it. I put it back, get dressed, and go downstairs.

The trouble with my dreams is this: I often can't really convince myself that they didn't happen. Of all the dreams I've had and been able to remember, I honestly can't say that they didn't really happen. A pale glow of belief remains.

Rhonda's doing her sphinx number on us this morning, not looking at us, let alone talking. She eats cereal at the table and leaves before I sit.

Dad's at his desk, lost in his bankbook and bills. Whenever I see him doing this, working carefully with his pen, my impression is of a man crossing a wobbly bridge.

Mom asks me to take out the garbage. Lugging it out to the garage, I'm thinking that a lot of other guys my age, from middle-income families would have gone hunting for an after-school job by now. Mom and Dad have never said anything about it; just keep up the good work in school, they say. So I do, but the thought nags. I picture Dad at his desk in there.

I held jobs the past three summers and didn't like any of them, the last one least of all, though I saved $500 for college. It was a dishwashing job at a downtown restaurant called The Cauldron. My partner in the steam and grease was a big dude named Clive who mumbled a lot and who I figured was illiterate. Mr. Stone, the old white guy who ran the place, yelled at Clive a lot, and Clive never said anything back. More often, though, Stone yelled at both of us—just came raving into the kitchen saying how slow we were and why weren't the glasses done. My employment ended the night I overheard him referring to us as "Amos 'n' Andy over there." I threw my apron at his feet and walked. If only I'd thrown it right in his bony face.

So that's me and jobs. But sometimes I think I've had it too easy, especially considering Dad and the things he had to do when he was young. In limiting my contact with life, I've missed the humble glories Dad gathered early. And I envy him—me, the lucky one.

I lower the garage door and look around. It's a still and shining day, a good day for a walk. But I won't be taking any walk. I'll stay here at home, the safest place. Seventeen years old, supposedly a few breaths short of manhood, and here I am, clinging to home. If this reflection bit any deeper I'd force myself to go once around the block, past the white faces and closed houses. But it doesn't, and with little else to do I go back inside to study math.

I'm at the dining-room table when the phone rings.

Mom answers, and I don't listen till I hear her say, "What?" There's a pause. "We'll stay here as long as we damn well . . ." Another pause. "Go to hell!" Mom hangs up.

I go to the kitchen and she's sitting, rubbing her temple.

Once when I was twelve I told Rhonda where to go and Mom whacked me.

"We've got some nice neighbors," she mutters. I put my hand on her shoulder, and she squeezes it. "You told 'em fine," I say.

Her hair's unbrushed and she looks more frayed than usual. My favorite picture of her was taken the day she graduated from Howard in 1961. She's there in her gown, arm in arm with Grandpa Morris and holding her diploma. She's smiling beautifully, her hair shoulder-length, and you'd swear it was Rhonda except that Mom looks so happy. Her degree was in education, but she married Dad after teaching for a year at a Baltimore grammar school. Then she worked intermittently until Fred Jr. was born, resumed after his death, and stopped for good when she had me.

The doorbell rings and it's the paper boy, a skinny white kid with a baseball cap. Mom goes to the door to pay him, and I go back to my homework. Through the window I see the kid scoot out of the driveway on his bike. A car drives by and I brace for the sound of breaking glass. It doesn't come, but I can't study anymore.

Mom doesn't tell Dad about the phone call.

For all her grudge and for all her time, Rhonda doesn't go to visit Wilbur's folks, and no one brings it up.

Sleep comes hard tonight. I can't shake that phone call. My insides boil as I lie here, and a few times I sit on the side of the bed, waiting to get tired. When at last I do, I drift off hoping for no dreams.

Tonight's dream is brief, at least. No one from school is in it, no McBride—just the family. The phone keeps ringing and Mom keeps answering it. Each time she hangs up she says that they're coming for us, we have to move fast. Dad and I rush around, gathering things to take. Then Rhonda's voice comes calmly from the porch: "They're here." There's shouting outside, and the kitchen window breaks.

A pithy sort of dream, not quite as fancy as last night's.

Back in the city, Rhonda and I sometimes accompanied Mom to Seven Angels Baptist Church on Sundays. Dad only went on Christmas Eve. Then my ears and knees got tired, in that order, and I stopped going. Soon Rhonda did too. Mom kept going regularly until a month before our move, when things got busy, and she hasn't gone since.

This morning she says she's going and tells Dad she needs the car. He looks a bit surprised, then hands her the keys and resumes reading the paper. I watch Mom go out, in her light-blue coat and flower-topped hat.

Like yesterday, there's no breeze outside—unusual for October—and sunlight gilds the leaves like cool fire. Dad and I watch a TV program on the history of the Olympics. Rhonda gets lunch ready, as Mom asked her to, then puts one of her Bob Marley albums on the stereo.

Mom gets back just before noon, and as she hangs her coat up, her expression seems faintly sad.

"How was it, dear?" Dad asks her.

"It was nice," she says. "I talked to the Hardings."

"Oh yeah?"

"They looked good. Zeke said the four of us should go out to dinner sometime. Louise White was there too."

"She talk you silly?"

"Not so bad. It was nice."

After lunch, Dad and I watch a football game, which I quit in the third quarter. I'm studying in the dining room and Mom's doing the dishes when she stops to put on a record she bought recently, Pachelbel's *Canon in D Major*. Though she played the flute as a teenager, Mom never listened much to classical music. But she heard this on an FM station and thought it was nice.

It is, but I don't want to hear it. Those violins gliding down and down, steep and sad. I can't listen well to classical music. With severe purity, it comes winding down from a past age, when different things mattered. And the facelessness of it, the lack of voices, makes me feel so small and lost. This is a sound more of nature than of humans, a weaving sound that seems to come from the sky, and I imagine mountains or oceans or misted forest valleys, all timeless. I listen and the present shrinks to nothing, along with me, and Mom and Dad and Rhonda, and McBride and Holly, and Jesse Jackson and the Klan and the President. Against an ocean, the human race suddenly seems a minor if noisy idea, a Creator's faded afterthought. A lover of this music would necessarily take some comfort from all that; I can't, not yet.

"That's so lovely," Mom says from the kitchen, sounding distant.

"Yeah, it is," I say. As soon as the record ends I go put Marley on again, and the reggae bobs up.

Back at my math book, I take comfort in Marley's lazy, looping voice at the music's center, as personal as sweat. It's the sound of one man, a single person, which is all I am.

After dinner a couple of Rhonda's friends come by in a car and she leaves with them. They're going to try again to see Wilbur at the hospital.

We're watching "60 Minutes" when we hear sirens from down the block. I go outside but can't see anything. When I come back in, Mom is dialing a number.

"Who you calling?" Dad asks.

"Maggie Chisholm," Mom says.

Mom holds the receiver and waits. Dad and I watch TV. Then I hear Mom: "Hello, Maggie? This is Beth. What's hap—Oh, no! . . . Okay, settle down. Take a breath, dear . . . But he's okay? Thank God."

Mom is quiet a long minute.

"Okay, Maggie. Just stay calm. You want me to come over? . . . Okay, I'll see you tomorrow. Don't worry, dear."

Dad turns the set down and we wait for Mom to return. Stepping into the room, she puts a hand on her hip and looks at Dad. "That man next door to them took a pot shot at Joe."

"You mean with a gun?" Dad says.

Mom nods.

"Jeez!" He grimaces.

98

"The police took him in," she says. "He's a nut. Joe wasn't hurt, but Maggie's scared out of her head. She's afraid he'll have a heart attack."

"Jeez," Dad mumbles again.

Mom sits, not bothering to turn the TV back up. "Poor Maggie," she says eventually. "And their poor boys. You know one of them, don't you, Luke?"

"Yeah, Nate," I say.

When Rhonda comes home after nine, Mom and Dad seem too weary to notice her. But I notice her, those blurred eyes. I think of asking, but then she's gone upstairs.

Gradually Dad emerges from his cloud of tired alarm and goes to turn up the TV. As he does I catch a look from him. I'm not sure what he sees in my face, but I can guess from what I see in his—that familiar, impatient pleading in his eyes. "Don't slide back into that pit of yours," they say. "You're young, boy. Please."

My mind's already shifted ahead, though, to tomorrow. I recall McBride on Friday—"I know I have to do something." And tomorrow we start out again, facing and dodging in a new level of fever. Up at Bently, the desks are waiting. Weekends are a blink.

Mom puts her record on again. That record—violins weave, steeper and sadder. Mists move through a valley of tall pines. An ocean rolls, and I feel lost.

October 5th

Rhonda stays home today. She's not feeling well.

At the bus stop I wait for Nate to show, trying to feel ready. When he appears he's tight-lipped, knotted at the core. The white kids, forming their cluster at the customary ten-foot distance, cast glances at him.

"How you doing?" I ask him.

"How do you think?" he mutters.

I look away, reaching for an approach. "The police have the guy, Nate. He's not going to try that again."

"Who says?" Nate glares. "The only way to make sure is to kill the sucker!"

A few white kids stare at us. Their group is smaller this morning; some faces are missing from it.

"You got the law behind you," I tell Nate, my voice low.

He doesn't look at me, not there or sitting next to me on the bus.

The cornerstone needs cleaning again, and this time the author's white-paint words are big and perfectly legible: "Run Nigger Run." More original, at least. The old janitor's there with his mop, bucket, and cloth, scrubbing as we near the entrance. He eyes us as if we were all foremen passing by, and scrubs. No hurry, man.

In homeroom there's a sprinkle of empty desks—six, according to Irwin's roll call. Behind me, one girl asks another in a whisper whether she's heard about Mrs. Hoffmann. And in the locker-side chatter before English I learn that Hoffman is out, hurt, in the hospital. Beaten up. I hear one black girl theorize that Jennie's city boyfriend did the job.

Jennie saunters down the hall—never any rushing for that girl. I'd forgotten she was due back. An uncounted factor—just what we need.

All through Mrs. Rollins's class, the thought of Hoffmann bruised and bloodied keeps drumming in my head. Hoffmann the statue. Hoffmann with the glasses. She's the one I could least have imagined it happening to, and I can't now.

Mrs. Rollins doesn't smile this morning, not once. She passes back test papers and reviews them in a clipped way. A white guy protests about an answer he got wrong, and she says okay, she'll change his mark. Then, instead of standing she sits behind her desk and goes over a story we're supposed to have read, but which almost no one has, judging from the lack of comments. Mrs. Rollins doesn't seem especially nervous, just listless, washed out, as she did after Friday's class. And as she reads to us, her hand plays gently with the white stone with the rose, as if it were a charm.

I more or less blow the test in math, making a few dumb mistakes which I don't realize till I've passed it in. I go up and ask Irwin if I can have it back for a minute. Sitting with fingers interlaced, he tells me he can't give a test back after it's been passed in. My irritation fades by the time I retake my seat.

There's a footnote floating around the halls. Tommy Kelly, the freshman who was beaten up three weeks ago, is not coming back. His parents have decided to move.

With the absences, the library's less full during study period. I sit alone, trying to read history. Jennie's in her corner, chair tilted back, gabbing with her friends. Hoffmann's substitute is a gangly young guy with a light mustache. He stands at the counter, looking around a lot but saying nothing as the talk picks up.

Nate is at Law's table again, talking. Whenever I see Law with his friends, he's seated in the middle, slouched, with arms crossed. The king and the king's men; the godfather and his soldiers. Same with Crown, come to think of it.

I look at the clock. How are you doing today, McBride?

I'm quicker in getting to McBride's class today, for some reason—maybe because the sight of me, before any harder faces, might do him good.

He sees me as I sit, and gives me a quick smile. For this moment I'm encouraged. He looks fitter, sharper, watching the kids arrive.

Crown comes in—bang, down in his seat.

Law enters, Nate behind him.

Others come. Then Monahan. "Hi, Oscuh," he says.

I tighten. McBride's expression is unchanged as Monahan sits beside Crown, who squints a grin.

Others enter, books going *whump* on desktops.

Jennie comes in, the last one.

My ears get ready. "Okay folks," McBride begins.

"Okay, Oscuh."

McBride's gaze jerks to Monahan. Already, the first shot—they're not wasting time.

"Terry, get up," McBride says evenly.

Monahan leers at Crown.

"Did you hear me? Stand up."

He rises, hands dangling at his sides. McBride goes to the head of the aisle. "Come with me," he says, and waits till Monahan clumps up to him before leading him out the door. Monahan sends a smirk back over his shoulder.

Chatter rumbles up through the room. I stare deep into the wood of McBride's desk, trying to make the talk fade, the time run.

I think of Crown over there, and Law in back, sprawled in their chairs as the talking continues at a low boil. Day after day they've sat like that, each on his own side, each feeling the heat of one pole rising around him—his to draw on if and when he dares. But that perception's wrong, I know now. They're stupid. They're at the same pole, Law and Crown—locked as one force, like in the dream. McBride is at the other pole.

And I think of Jennie back there, big-eyed and languid in that tattered green top. I hope she's too foggy to grasp what she's done and feel tickled. Her words echo— "Ohhh, Oscar, I really don't know." Simple, funny. But my memory hears them now as an opening rocket, a signal. Nice work, Jennie. If you knew any history, maybe you'd feel like Lexington, like Fort Sumter.

Recalling how McBride used to seem in front of us, I wonder if the hard ones sensed something—that crack —well before I did, and were just waiting. Waiting on the monster.

To my left, Nate rests his chin on his forearms. McBride returns without Monahan and the talking stops. As he turns to us briskly I see him exhale deeply, his eyes determined.

"All right," he says. "Before that interruption, this is what I was going to say. Things have not been as they should be in this class."

My hand clenches.

"This is partly my fault," he goes on.

No, don't give them that! Come down like metal, Oscar.

"But it's going to be different. We're getting behind in the material, and a few people are making trouble for the rest of us. So as of now, that's going to change."

There's clear silence as he picks up the textbook from his desk and turns the pages. The pride I feel is tentative, snagged on disappointment. That was good, but couldn't he have said more? Wilbur and now Hoffmann, after all . . .

"Let's move on to the last stage of the Revolution," he says.

Well, he did okay. He has a class to teach, and maybe it was enough. And Monahan, the little bastard, is out of here. I open my book and smile inside, tentatively. Back to Franklin and Washington, rebels and redcoats.

"By 1780," he begins, "the war's main theater had switched to the southern colonies, and things weren't going well at all for the Americans. The British general, Howe, had been replaced—by who?"

He points to a white guy up front. "Cornwallis" comes the answer, and McBride is rolling, his cadence back like Lazarus.

"At the same time, various guerrilla leaders were carrying out raids against . . ." He halts, looking toward the back. "Jennie?"

Jennie is leaning toward Law, talking.

"Jennie," McBride repeats, firmly.

"What?" she says.

"Save it for lunch period, okay?"

"Save what?"

"Never mind. Tell me about what Cornwallis did."

She leans back. "I don't know nothin' 'bout—"

"You ought to, Jennie. Pay more atten—"

"Don't care 'bout this damn stuff," she mutters.

"You better start caring about it," McBride says. He lets a moment pass. "Now, American guerrilla leaders at this time were—"

"Ain't listenin' to no half-breed."

The class goes still. Mouths open, eyes dart. Jennie's utterance hangs above us as McBride stands there. His lips part, he eyes go small as wrinkles pull his face into the mask of a man kicked, a man speared. For an endless minute, no sound comes out of him. And Jennie slouches there, trading a lazy look with Law.

Then McBride's gaze lowers to his book and seems to burn through it. "Yes," he mutters. He looks at the class again, as he might look into a deep cave. Then he continues. "The British went north . . . north through the

108

Carolinas. And they beat Greene . . . a couple of times they defeated him.''

When the bell sounds I leave quickly. My skin squirms with the old ache, and I'm thinking that before, McBride was merely stuck, having trouble in summoning the dormant thing I hoped was there. Now he might be a cripple. That face was a crippled face. And all it took was a word.

Nate finds me at lunch. I've taken a new table near the entrance, far from the teachers.

"Why you sitting here?" he asks.

"I like it here."

He puts his tray down. His gaze is steady, and there's something behind it set to jump out. "I been wanting to talk to you," he says.

"Yeah?"

"I been thinking, you and me been on the fence like a couple of pussies while all this shit's been going on."

"You think so, huh?" I mumble.

"Yeah, that's what I think." He glares. "It's time we picked our own side, man. Start fighting back."

I put my fork down but don't look at him. "Tell me about sides. How many you think we got?"

"What do you mean? You been sleeping?"

Now I look at him. "No, I got eyes."

"All right," he says. "So it's this—it's a choice of being a nigger or being a man."

"So how do we be a man?"

"George Law says we can hang out with him and his gang. They stick together. They don't take nothing."

"Yeah, they're men."

"And we're not. Not until we start sticking together and standing our ground. My father got shot at. You got your window smashed. It's war now."

Explanations use up breath, and breath is something I value. So I shake my head.

Nate's face sharpens the way it did a week ago in this cafeteria, when he said he wanted to waste Crown. Only now it's for me. "Shit, you're getting as white as they are!" he says. "You been hanging around too much with that white bitch."

"Shut up. You don't know her."

He takes his tray and gets up. "Have fun with your lily-ass friends." Then he leaves.

As his words ring, a doubt edges into me. I recall Wilbur's offer of strength in numbers, an option that was knocked senseless along with him. Having missed that train, I've now chosen to miss another, deliberately stranded myself. Nate's call to arms, however crazy it sounded and however definite my no, makes me wonder which of us is actually being smarter and more tuned-in. Especially since there's no way of telling how much more irrational things will get. When the shit really hits, maybe Nate will be better off because he decided that numerical strength is the answer. Lofty ideas like "being your own man" — maybe they're the first to end up under the steamroller at times like this.

Then I see Nate over with Law's gang, stretching his neck like a fidgety court minister to hear whatever Law's mumbling, and the doubt is gone.

I eat mechanically, thinking of Holly.

Experiment day with Walker. I ignite the Bunsen burner, and Holly gingerly places a filled beaker above it. She's looking extra nice, her dark hair glossy, her figure fine in a red sweater, and it's as if all the ache has rushed below my waist. I'm having trouble concentrating on anything but her. I think Cameron has picked this up, judging from the arsenic glance I just got. Burn in hell, Cameron.

Walker, chin up, makes his rolling circuit of the room. "Remember," he says, "don't let it boil too long."

I look at Holly and she's watching bubbles form. We've hardly spoken yet.

"So how were the hills?" I ask.

"Fine, beautiful," she smiles, then looks back at the bubbles. I do too.

"Too bad about Mrs. Hoffmann," I say.

"I know," she says quietly. "I never liked her all that much, but God. Poor lady." She turns a page of the workbook. "I keep . . . I keep waiting for it to level off somehow."

I'm conscious now of a desire to share something with Holly other than sighs and laments. I want to stare into her, to talk from inside and hear her answer straight. I want something real from her. And I'm not patient.

"A guy just told me I ought to join George Law's bunch."

"Who said that?"

"Nate Chisholm. His father got shot at yesterday."

"I don't know him."

111

In the beaker, bubbles start streaming to the top.

"It just doesn't make sense," Holly mutters.

That's a comment you usually hear when some nut-case shoots a famous person or when children die, and it always annoys me a little. It's the uselessness of it, the implied idea that everything ought to add up. But I hold my stare on her lowered eyes, wanting her to feel all I feel.

"You know what Jennie Davis called McBride in history?"

"No," she says, shaking her head. "And I'd rather not know." She looks up, and I'm shocked to see her eyes shining. "Luke, I just hate all this. I mean, I hear my friends talking crazy. I pass black kids in the hall and I can't look at them. Every day I feel like crying."

We both look down at the blue flame.

"And there's just nothing we can do about it," she says. "You don't know how bad I feel."

The solution boils, fighting with itself. Bubbles gurgle and burst; steam rises.

After that we just mumble to each other about which step is next, and we're the last to complete the experiment, just as the bell goes off. By the time we've put everything away, the hall traffic has all but stopped. I leave first, but Holly catches up to me by the stairs.

"Luke," she says, touching my elbow.

I turn, and she looks flustered, lost for words.

"I'm really sorry," she murmurs. Quickly she kisses my cheek and leaves.

As I hurry to Spanish, there's a resentment in me—not at Holly, not exactly. I can't really blame her. All I wish is that she hadn't been oblique about it. If she'd come out with it plain I'd have felt sorry, but also maybe smiled and nodded. It would probably have been a relief, and wouldn't have left me feeling somehow cheated. I would have forfeited the kiss to have heard her say it straight.

Hoffmann's gangly substitute — Mr. Page, he informs us — asks where we left off last week, and someone tells him. He reads haltingly, pausing at times to figure out some pronunciation. His face suggests a worried weasel, though without any intentness, and after several fumbled replies to his fumbled questions, he goes to the tape recorder and turns on a tape of Spanish songs: "See if you can pick out the lyrics." Kids glance dully at each other and sink onto their elbows as guitars start up and foreign tongues flash. A party song, it sounds like. Taking Hoffmann's desk, Page rests a long leg on the rung of a stool and plays with a pen. It's a long period.

Headed for my locker afterward, I spot Barry walking ahead of me. During class I noticed him slouched in a seat in a rear corner — no small feat on my part, since he's hard to notice in a full room. He turns down another corridor, and I'm about to look away when he drops a book. As he bends to get it, a foot kicks it away. It's then that I see Law, Powers, Nate, and three others. They're leaning back along a windowsill, watching Barry. Still bent, Barry looks and says something, then grabs the book and hurries on. So do I.

After I've been to my locker, I make for the library. To get there, I realize, I have to pass Law's checkpoint; I hope they've left. They haven't. Striding by, I feel their eyes. For an instant I see Law in the corner of my vision, and Nate beside him.

There are a few more kids than usual in the library, studying or just sitting as Mrs. Wells waddles around the shelves. But the noise of the halls is distant, the peace blessed. A minute after I sit, Barry comes in, stiff-shouldered. I catch his eye, but he looks away and takes a table along the opposite wall. He's waiting for the bus too, probably, though his home's only half as far as mine. If he only knew how I turned down Nate's offer of manhood.

I don't get far with studying, and end up absorbing sunlight from the window. I touch my cheek where Holly planted her lips, and dismiss the thought of her. Outside it's brisk and breezy, good for walking. Good for walking home. But here I wait for the protective yellow shell of the bus to rumble me back like a third-grader. Should I let uncertain shadows rob me of my right to walk home? I wrestle with this till three, when the bus arrives.

Barry gets on ahead of me. I go to sit near the front, but seeing him in back, I head down there.

"How ya doing?" I ask him.

A bit startled, he shoves over and I sit. "Not bad," he says. "How 'bout you?"

"Surviving."

The bus grinds out. As in the library, there are a few more kids than usual, a fairly even number of black and white.

We've gone almost a block and I'm looking out the window when I see that red car by the curb. Crown, Toohey, and the others are there, leaning against it. I stop looking. "How'd you like Hoffmann's sub?" I ask Barry.

114

He smiles crookedly. "What's his name again?"

"Page."

"How'd you like those songs?"

"Loved 'em. Can't wait to get to Spain."

Two stop signs from Cedar Drive, I wonder whether I should mention seeing that business with Law. But Barry, as usual, doesn't seem at ease. He's all rumpled-looking, with books layered on his lap. Bringing up the incident might make him more nervous.

"Nice day," I say.

"Yeah, too bad we had to waste it back there."

We pull onto Cedar and stop; I get up to let him out.

"Well, see ya in gym," he says.

"Yup."

Moving on, I watch Barry do down the sidewalk to the hedge-bordered house with rust shingles. Yeah, see you in gym. You and Toohey and Lattanzio and the locker room.

When I get home, Mom says, "Hi, dear" without looking at me. Then she breathes a complaint about not being able to find a pen to write to Aunt Donna, asks me to take out the garbage, and goes off to dig through the dining-room bureau.

Upstairs I call the cops to ask about the lead I gave them. After a brief hold the sergeant comes on and explains that Toohey simply said he'd *heard* about our window. No evidence. Sorry, he says. As for Wilbur's case, questioning yielded zero—Toohey and company had alibis—and "the investigation is proceeding."

Returning to the kitchen, I make a sandwich, pour a glass of orange soda, and sit at the table. It dawns on me that I haven't thought of McBride at all for two hours straight, probably in the interest of not feeling worse. This is the first time, I believe, that I've been fully aware of having such an ability, this talent for choosing what to think or not to think about.

Mom returns to check a drawer. "Gonna see about that garbage?" she says.

"Soon as I finish this," I reply.

She finds a broken pencil and flicks it back in the drawer.

"Mom?" I say.

"Mm?"

"Do you know if our family has any white blood?"

She glances up, quizzical, but keeps rummaging. "They say we all have some." She shrugs, and shuts the drawer. "Those overseers weren't too particular." Then she heads upstairs, just as Rhonda enters the kitchen.

Rhonda pours a glass of soda and sits at the table too. Her hair is tangled and she's in her stocking feet.

"How you feeling?" I ask.

"Okay."

I finish my sandwich and down the soda. "What's with Mom?" I ask.

She puts her glass down. "I guess some white man said something to her at the supermarket."

The heat rushes through me, hotter than anytime before. I feel it as I take the garbage out, and when I lower the garage door, I punch a panel hard. I feel it through the evening and hardly notice Dad when he comes in. I feel it at supper and while trying to do my homework. I feel it in bed.

October 6th

As Rhonda and I walk to the bus stop, there's the far-off thought that this will be one of the pictures I'll most remember through the years — these wordless walks, before the sun takes hold, to our little pavement limbo. The image of Mom in her housecoat fades behind me. White kids arrive and wait.

Nate appears just before the bus does, and doesn't look at me or speak. After I get on, he sits in back, by himself. Rhonda's the last to get on — moving slowly this morning. Crossing my legs, I close my eyes as we start to move, and it's a moment before I realize that Rhonda has sat with me. Chin in my hand, I look at her, then out the window, unable to recall the last time she chose to sit next to me on a school bus or anywhere except the family car. And there's something else. That graceful shape of her face, the eyes and profile that have always made me think of a queen — they're somehow softer, her gaze at once more outward and inward. And that compression of her lips, the lips that even without moving have said so many final things, is gone. She holds her books in what looks like a delicate embrace.

I glance at her again. She's staring straight ahead, and

119

pity starts to open in me, a dark pity for this girl I suddenly feel to be my sister. Then it stops, and I look out at the passing lawns. As quickly as it began the feeling fades, as memories of her former face return like a cold echo. So now she's decided to sit with me.

The old janitor's busy again out front. He's certainly been earning his pay. This morning, for a change, it's an antiwhite slogan—"Kill Whitey"—and the paint is yellow. The cornerstone, with that dignified "1963" carved into it, will get faded with all this scrubbing.

Reaching the doors, I get a look from the janitor, whom I've never really regarded closely before. He's a white guy with a frayed cap, rail-straight, his face a web of wrinkles. Maybe because of the wrinkles, his mouth stays open a bit, showing stained teeth. As soon as he sees me he looks at the wall, scrubbing, as though I've caught him leaving a message rather than removing one. I wonder how long he's worked here.

Irwin's roll call, that slow-motion tennis game, reveals a few more absences than yesterday. Another one turns up in English—Mrs. Rollins. In her place is a smartly dressed black lady with wary ways, a Miss Bradley. Reviewing Fitzgerald with efficiency, she watches us like a warden and demands attention several times, including mine: "You over there, mind waking up a little?"

I straighten up slightly, still thinking of Mrs. Rollins. At least *she's* out of the picture, if temporarily—at home, perhaps picking daisies while dreaming on Henry James.

Next period, Irwin's chalk-tap is distant as I think of Mom's encounter at the supermarket. I construct the bloodless face of the man who "said something to her" —a man I'll probably never meet. I meet him in my mind while Irwin drones. Yes: a bloated, bloodless face that I spit in, then belt with an open hand. Then I kick him in the middle of his pus-gut.

I take my time getting to gym, and when I get there, most of the others are changed and gone. Holding his clipboard, Lattanzio stands in the narrow hall outside the locker room. "Hustle!" he calls. "Come on, Parrish, get changed. We're going outside."

Going outside? I twirl my locker combination and pull my clothes off. So far, as I said, Lattanzio's policy has been laissez-faire. I like it that way.

When I get out to the athletic field, the other guys are crowded around Lattanzio as he assigns sides, a football tucked against his big ribcage. Listening to him, I find something new besides his tactics. His commands used just to tell us what to do; now there's an earnestness to them, a touch of how he was when he caught Toohey and Shaw fighting. I often feel that my guesses about people might be just that — half-baked guesses; but in the brown nuggets of his eyes I think I see a tiny light of mission, a fumbling purpose. As he runs names off alphabetically from the clipboard, a reflection forms in me — fully, at last — about how, in the heat, we all squirm into shapes that are strange to us. I wish I knew mine better.

"Parrish!"

"Yup?"

"You're with them." He points to the left, where a half-dozen guys are standing. I join them, my legs getting cold.

"Nelson." Without surprise, I observe that Lattanzio's alphabet is flexible. The two teams, in this largely

121

white class, are getting an even sprinkle of blacks—four and four.

"Toohey," Lattanzio calls, and Toohey steps over to the edge of the group I'm in. He gives a sickly smile to his fat friend, who has yet to be called. Two other whites are sent to opposite sides, and the fat one remains.

"Yeager." He goes to the other side, where his wide form obscures Barry, who stands spindly and silent. Lattanzio marks the end zones, designates quarterbacks—a white for theirs, a black for ours—then flips a coin. We get the ball first.

"Remember, this is touch, not tackle," Lattanzio says.

With the ball's first snap the chill air is banished and we're running, yelling, grappling in the sun. For the first three plays I block left, covering a stout black guy who proves easy enough. Lattanzio, with his board and whistle, stands to the side like a bear on sentry duty. Bear—another cliché he fits. "That's it!" he bellows. "Penetrate! Toohey, watch those elbows!"

Our quarterback, a stringbean bus-in kid with an afro, sends two clean passes to a fast white kid. But on the next play the other team intercepts. They push us back ten yards, then I cut in through a space and tag the quarterback for a loss.

"All right, Parrish!" Lattanzio calls, and I feel good.

Next they send Barry out for a pass, but the ball brushes his fingers and drops. Eyes down, he returns to the huddle. They exhaust their downs and turn the ball over to us.

In the huddle, I look over and see Toohey facing me. I give him my stare and he looks down.

"Parrish," the quarterback says, "block and count to three, then slip left, head out, and cut across." He traces the pattern on his palm. "I'll hit you in the right corner. You guys cover me good."

We break; I crouch. Hike, snap. One two three—I slip left, charge out and then right. The ball comes sailing and I jump, snag it, and turn to run. In the next instant my back is whacked hard, and I nearly yell. Twisting around, I see Yeager lumbering away, and he looks back with a little smile.

"Nice going," the stringbean tells me.

My back stings as I join the huddle.

Two plays later, the fast white kid gets the handoff and rushes in for a touchdown.

Our quarterback sends a strong throw return, which their quarterback catches but doesn't get far with. On their third down, at midfield, Stringbean intercepts and makes a good run. The mud flies for two more plays, with little headway. Then, in the huddle, I'm told to slip fast and go straight for a bomb. I wait tensely for the snap, then go. I'm clear in a second, and the pigskin lands neat and hard in my arms. Before I can accelerate, a shadowy hulk plows into my right side, knocking the ball from my hands and the wind from my chest. My shirt is grabbed and I'm thrown off-balance. Falling, I see Yeager above me. I leap up at Lattanzio's whistle.

"What the fuck you doing!" I yell.

"Tagging you, stupid."

"Hold it!" Lattanzio comes running up with everyone else. "When I blow the whistle, everything stops!"

"He tried to tackle me," I say.

"Tackle him—jeez!" Yeager sneers. "If I tackled him, he'd know it."

"He did, coach!" Stringbean says. "He tried to—"

"All right, all right!" Lattanzio waves his clipboard. "Ease up, Yeager. The pass is good; take it from there." He heads back to the side, shaking his head. "Friggin' crazies. Can't play a decent game."

The teams filter back to huddle. I pick the ball up and watch Yeager walking away, looking over his shoulder. "Nigger fairy," he mutters.

My stomach burns. Rejoining my team, I see Toohey smile over at Yeager, and Yeager smiles back.

On the snap, Stringbean fakes, then scrambles into the end zone.

The game goes on, our ragged lines pushing back and forth. But I'm no longer part of it. They get a touchdown, but the whistle ends it; we win, 14–7.

As it happens, the white guys head inside almost as a body. Yeager and Toohey walk in together, talking in low voices and smiling. Barry brings up the rear, not smiling and not looking back. I watch him to the doors.

"Hurry it up," says Lattanzio, who scoops up the ball. He looks like he has a cramp in some vital organ.

I follow with the others.

"Good game," says Stringbean.

Inside, towel in my lap, I wait till the showers are mostly clear before going in.

I make no real attempt to feel ready for McBride's class. The shower helped some, but my insides still quiver.

And the thing I hate is the sense of inevitability, buzzing like flies in the preclass chatter — a question more of "when and who" than of "what if." When will the rupture occur, and who will be the spark? Jennie, that hazy-eyed harpy? Or Monahan, with that toothy grin? George, his arms crossed coolly? Or Crown, who's mostly been quiet, possibly waiting? It's as if the kids have shifted as a single mind to believing that none of it can be avoided, none of what's been happening or waiting to happen.

McBride isn't here yet. Nate has taken a seat in back, near Law and Jennie.

McBride comes in, tosses a folder onto his desk, and squints at us. Then he raises a hand for quiet. "Okay," he says. "We're coming to the end of the Revolution and I'd like to wrap it up. So before we move on to Yorktown, let's review the ideas behind independence."

So he's off, on a review I don't consider necessary. We've covered this area pretty thoroughly. Not only that, but his voice sounds empty, whereas before it was calmly charged with importance. Talking has started in back.

"Could you pipe down back there?" he snaps, raising his hand again. They stop.

"It was the idea, expressed before but never acted upon in a major way, that every man had certain basic rights and freedoms . . ."

Yeah, yeah. Pursuit of happiness, pursuit of happiness. But at least nothing's happened yet. Count the minutes to the bell's reprieve.

"Now the ideals translated to the war by Paine had roots in France and England. What French philosopher still alive then was a major influence?'' He points to a smart white girl.

"Rousseau," she says.

"Right, and in England, a century before?" He squints around the room. "Nate?"

Carefully I look over my shoulder. Nate is still, eyes darting from side to side. Then he shrugs.

"No?" McBride says, then looks to me. "Luke?"

"Locke," I say.

"Yes, John Locke," he says.

"You see that?" comes a voice from in back. "Luke understands it when you talk white." Law—he's done with waiting.

"Quiet, George," McBride snaps.

"Don't ask Nate nothing, he don't talk white." The titters start. "Just ask Luke the questions; he talks just like you."

McBride's stare and stillness kill the chuckles. He stares at Law. "Shut up, George. Shut up."

"See, man?" George speaks. "I don't get a word you're saying."

"You talk so *white* Oscar." Jennie now.

I haven't been looking at them, and their voices seem disembodied, coming from the air. McBride stares. There's a slight tremor along his shoulders as he takes a breath, and for a second I wonder—for the hundreth time, but with darker chill—how much he can take.

"*You* talk *stupid*," he says.

Jennie's chuckle hits the air like a bubble. McBride stands—half living, half stone. Then, with another deep breath, his features sag back to normal in what I sense is a willed transference of inner weight.

126

"All right," he says, "Rousseau and Locke. Rousseau viewed government as an artificial force against nature, robbing men of freedoms they'd have in natural state. Locke . . ."

His speech, more chiseled and stately than ever, comes from a hollow place, and I'd rather not listen. On the other side, Crown and Monahan leer to each other.

When class ends, McBride turns toward his desk. Passing close, I nearly reach out and pat his arm. In the hall, I think how much they'd have loved to see that, the fresh ammo it would have given them.

It occurs to me while picking through lunch that McBride could have used his state-given power as a teacher to evict Law and Jennie, but didn't. These omissions of his no longer affect me as they did; I puzzle over them for a minute, then forget them.

Rhonda's with the Wilbur crowd, seated between two boys. No doubt they've asked, with proper concern, why she wasn't here yesterday. Well, Rhonda's taken care of. In them she has shelter, and that's lucky.

In chemistry I take the seat by the door and Cameron sits with Holly. My courtesy, Cameron; enjoy it, you jackass. Once, while Walker lectures, I think I see Holly turn and look toward me.

There's some excitement in the halls between periods when someone starts a fire in the boys' lavatory. Lattanzio, whose study period has just ended, charges in with an extinguisher and has it out in a minute. "Everybody get to class," he exhales when he comes out. As the crowd breaks, I look back to see him talking with the old janitor, and I feel for an instant the frustration of a man whose code relies on simple precision and strength — the frustration that an extinguisher can't be used on anything but fire.

Spanish class. As we come in, Page stands rubbing his mustache with one finger. At his side is a projector. The film is called *Holiday in Mexico City*, and for the next forty minutes we sit washed in the noise and color of open markets, sombreroed dancers, and Mexican smiles. But I must admit that it's nice with the lights out, the shades down.

Bumping out the door, I notice Barry behind me and let him come alongside.

"Hell of a movie, huh?" I say.

"Yup." He sort of smiles.

Nearing the intersecting hall where Barry's locker is, I ask if he heard about the fire. He says he was wondering what the commotion was.

We separate to go to our lockers. Barry's probably headed for the library again to wait for the bus, and as I take out my text and notebooks, I realize I don't want to follow him there. Holding my jacket, I gaze down the rapidly emptying hall to the exit sign. Pictures of the past nine days rush through me, starting with the broken window, and a creeping shame takes over. For so long I've wanted to be stronger than I feel. That was the wish I threw onto McBride's shoulders, only to find them already sagging with a burden of their own. I've hated this sense of fragility all the more since I began to realize what the stakes can be for one person alone. Now I think of Dad's life and Mom at the supermarket and suddenly see that this is a testing time, a time to be brave. It's a test I might be busy flunking. But I have to take it.

There's a feeling of freedom as I step out and the air hits me. A time to be brave. Dad was, and his father was; now I will be.

Striding down the driveway, I decide to take a short cut across the athletic field. The building's shadow falls on me as I walk behind the bleachers, and along the wall I discover a carnival of graffiti, mostly hate. "Nigger Go Home"—a white spray-painted swirl over a green "Kill Whitey." "Spades Die," says a red message further on, and under that, "Blow Up the Nigger Bus." "Sara C. Fucks Anybody" reads a white blurb. Whether the janitors know it or not, they have a big job ahead of them. Abruptly I'm nervous.

Reaching the other side of the bleachers, I step back into the sun. And there, approaching from my left, is Yeager, with two buddies behind him.

"Hey, monkey!" he calls, and I'm headed quickly away, in the direction of the street. I hear them hurrying up behind me. I won't run; I won't run.

"Hey, fuckin' spade!"

I burst inside and whirl to face them. "What, shit-head?"

Yeager's fist drives into my ribs and I'm down, my books scattered. I jump up, grab him by the collar, and shove, but one of the others kicks me in the hip and I buckle. Yeager knees me down. "Want your head smashed, nigger?"

As I look up at him my hands are claws, and I imagine a large wedge of flesh missing from the side of his neck.

The one who kicked me stands beside Yeager, arms braced, while the other waits to one side, smoking a cigarette.

"Come on," Yeager puffs. "I'll kick your black fairy ass."

I'm motionless. The kid beside him kicks my history book away.

"Go to hell," I say, and his fist hits my cheek, rolling me.

Holding my cheek, ears ringing, I glare up into his round, small-lipped, small-eyed face.

"Don't tell *me* nothing, monkey," he says.

Just then I notice, some twenty yards beyond them, two figures walking past—Cameron and a friend of his, both in their jock jackets. They're looking over, going past.

"I see you 'round here again, I'll pound the shit outa you," Yeager says.

Slowly the three of them turn away, the kicker stepping on a notebook.

I rise as they move off, and carefully gather my books. My face hurts, and my hip and ribs hurt.

Moving quickly toward the street, I'm shaking. I reach the sidewalk and stand there still shaking. Then I feel a laugh start to rise—so much for short cuts, I think. Oppressed—that's what I am, an oppressed black boy right out of *Roots*. A small cliché in a grand spray-painted cliché—"Nigger Go Home Kill Whitey Spades Die." And Yeager—Jesus, there's a fat-pig cliché. I touch my cheek. Clichés can punch.

The laugh dies before it comes, replaced by a sudden exhilaration as I realize I'm a victim, with a victim's bruise. Wounded by injustice, one soldier in a righteous fight. This, it occurs to me, must be a touch of what Rhonda has felt each day since her intellect began stirring, a brush of what Wilbur felt . . .

With a shudder, the sickness returns. I stare at the back of my hand, the deep brown. All my life I've tried to think of this color as something incidental, not a source of shame or pride or status or unknown doom or anything. That it was the color of Frederick Douglass, Martin Luther King, and my parents seemed abstract. But I feel I'm seeing and understanding it for the first time. It means something more serious than I've ever considered, something that has to be faced. How could I have hoped to escape it? How, looking through broken glass, and how, amid all the white faces? Awake now, finally, feeling dead. Maybe Rhonda, in the grim lines she drew in her speeches, was right all along.

I've been standing here for a few minutes now and need to move. I turn toward home, then halt, looking back at the school.

McBride is bent over papers when I come in and close the door. I must have done it quietly, because it takes him a moment to notice me. When he does, his face freezes. "Luke, what hap—" Then he looks down again and his arms fall to his lap. "Have a seat."

I pull up a desk and sit, slouching way back.

"Are you all right?"

I nod. "Don't ask me why I'm here," I say. " 'Cause I don't know."

He rubs his eyes. "I have some idea." He puts two fingers to his temple, and I wait for him to speak. It's a while. "You know, Luke, I've been in worse places and situations than this . . ." He pauses. "Well, at least as bad."

"I know," I say. "I haven't."

"Yes," he breathes. "I didn't think you had."

"What was it like?"

My voice is flat, jabbing, but I don't care. And his return stare is calm, as if he'd expected the question.

"Same sort of things happening," he says. "Same old words being used. Good people getting hurt." He starts to swivel a bit in his chair, side to side, as I wait. "There was always the feeling that one thing, one action, could make it better somehow. And every time, I tried to be the person who'd do it. I mean, why not me?" Slowly he chews his bottom lip, eyes now distant. "So I'd try . . . and I'd fail . . . But I always felt I'd missed by just this much. The right words, the right insight or approach or whatever would turn it all around. So I'd keep trying, and I'd get burned, and nothing seemed to really change. But as bad as it was . . ." His hand closes and he stares at it. "That sense hung on—that one individual could get the damn response . . . if only."

He pauses again, thumping his fingers, and takes a long breath. "New York . . . that was the worst. I made my speeches, all that high-flown stuff about cutting off the chain of hate. Once, in the middle of one of those, I got hit on the head with an eraser. Gave them a good laugh."

A corner of his mouth turns up, but he looks as though

he's swallowed something bitter. That's how I feel. And though his speech is slow and clear, there's a flatness to it that matches my own, a tightness like Wilbur's. Now I'm not sure I want him to keep talking, but he does.

"There was one kid—Tyler was his name. Lively boy. Quite a mouth on him. One day I grabbed him by the shoulders and just yelled and shook. He and his friends met me after school . . ." He stops, sighs a big sigh. "They even took my watch. Tyler," he repeats, as I know his memory has—many times. This may not be New York, but little besides the names has changed.

He stops swiveling, leans forward. "I'm going to talk to Mr. O'Donnell about having an assembly. All the kids in the school, all the teachers, to take this thing head-on."

"When?" I ask.

"I don't know. Soon."

Then, gradually, his gaze draws back from wherever it was and he looks at me. "Are you sure you're okay? I think the nurse is still in the building."

"It's just a bruise," I say. Then I get up. "Thank you," I tell him, and walk to the door.

He speaks again as I open it. "You know something funny, Luke?"

I turn. "What?"

"Mr. Everett, the one who teaches biology—he's in some hot water. One of his classes is going on a field trip, and he told them, 'Bring in the permission slips from your parents, or write yourselves one.' Some parents heard about it and made a fuss."

I smile and my cheek hurts.

He smiles at his blotter. "He's taking some heat. The trip may be canceled. It's just so funny." And he laughs. It's an off-key, unnatural laugh.

I hold the smile. "Thank God they're on their toes."

"Yeah." He nods, the chuckle thinning. "Yup. See you, Luke." He picks up a paper and leans back.

The bus has left, and my going-home steps are quick, my eyes alert.

When I come into the kitchen, Mom turns from the sink and sighs. "Oh, good!" she says. "Rhonda was worried when you weren't on the—"She sees my cheek. "Honey, what happened?"

"I had some trouble," I say.

"Damn!" she nearly shouts, and gets a damp cloth. I hold it to my face and sit. "Listen," she says, "from now on you wait for that bus! It's too risky—"

"I know, I know. I will."

Mom dries a dish and nearly drops it. "Damn white trash," she mutters.

Dad is rumbling when he gets home, rumbles through dinner, then sticks his face in the newspaper. Mom gets it out of him: at lunch hour he got into an argument about race with a white coworker. He doesn't notice my little mark.

I don't have much homework. Doing my lab report, I stop to flick dirt from the edges of pages in my chem book.

October 7th

Going to bed early had its benefits, but I'm sore as I fumble around in the bathroom, and I realize that the soreness will be a reminder, through the day, of yesterday. But everything feels too immediate for that to matter. My mind's already at school; I'm just going to follow it there. I eat hardly any breakfast, and so does Rhonda. Our good-byes to Mom sound empty.

Again Nate says nothing to me, and stands farther away; being clued in to this by now, I don't look at him. On the bus he goes to the rear again, by himself, and again Rhonda sits with me. Halfway to school she asks what's with Nate and me, and I shrug. Almost there, she asks how my face feels and I tell her okay. So now she's concerned about my bruises. Will wonders ever cease?

No job for the old janitor today — not at the cornerstone, at least, where only a yellow stain remains. Good; the guy needs a rest.

The same absences unfold from Irwin's roll call. Smart kids, I think. Why is it, I ask myself, that Law or Crown or any of those others has declined to add to the truancy rate? I answer myself immediately — coming here must be what they live for. There's a buzz going that Irwin collared a white guy writing something on his board just before anyone else came in, and took him to the office. Cal Irwin, warrior against racism.

It isn't till the first bell that my memory flips to what McBride said about an assembly. "Soon," he said. How soon?

Miss Bradley continues to cement her authority in English, lecturing us on paying attention and complaining when it's apparent that few have read today's story. I earn a "Very good" from her when I answer a question.

In math I feel sharp for once, as time lurches toward history. Irwin gives us back our tests; he's a fast corrector. I got a 78, C-plus. The clock on the wall looks like a robot's face, telling time matter-of-factly. I started off calmer than expected this morning; now I'm not so calm.

Walking to the library for study period, I pass Holly.

"Hi," she says.

"Hello."

I catch a sad, searching glance from her. Turning a corner, I look back to watch her slight body moving down the hall, losing itself in the stream of other bodies. It would be interesting to know her mind, but it's best to forget it. And by the time I'm in the library, I have.

Page presides again, content with the accomplishment of standing with his arm propped on a shelf. Talk is steady. Law's table is full, including Jennie and a couple of her friends, and Nate. More than once I hear McBride's name spoken. Once Jennie's eyes turn in my direction, and I look into my book.

"Yeah, great student," someone says. "Fine young man."

I can't tell whether it was Law or Powers, but snickers

follow. The talking intensifies with the minute hand's pull toward eleven. It's awfully hard to sit, and I'd rather be in gym, shooting baskets by myself. But when I next look up, there's a minute to go. Fourth period gapes, and McBride is waiting. Same as each of the past ten days, and I'm tired of it. Tired, and almost wishing for some final explosion.

Bell.

I'm going down a stairwell when I pass Rhonda. Our eyes meet and she looks vaguely anxious, as though asking me to stop for just a moment. I brush by with no word. And no expression, I hope.

There's the door, coming at me. I'm in, among the first arrivals, and I feel bars come down, *clang*, behind my back. It will be over in an hour, I tell myself, but at the moment that's a useless thought.

McBride's behind his desk, and as I sit at mine he looks up. "Hi, Luke."

"Morning," I say.

The usual parade spills in, minus a few — the shiny and the scruffy, the cowed and the loud. Aren't I getting poetic? Crown and Monahan, Jennie and Law, then Nate. And to burn a minute, I wonder what lurks today within the principal actors, what they carry here this time. In the case of the aforementioned it's an easy guess. Not so easy in the case of that man behind the desk, the man with the crack, who yesterday seemed to talk to me from the bottom of himself.

Law passes my seat. "Hi, boy."

As stragglers enter, McBride gets to his feet. "Today we wrap up this section of the book."

"Well all right!" Jennie chirps. Laugh, laugh.

"Glad you like it," McBride says, and goes to the map stand, which is turned to the map of the Revolution. "Now toward the latter part of 1781, Cornwallis moved into Virginia to get closer to the main British base in New York. Washington and Lafayette—"

"Come on!" Monahan comes to life. "Hurry, Oscar, hurry!"

McBride's glare suspends the giggles, but before he can speak, Jennie looks over at Monahan. "That's *my* line, shithead."

Monahan seems startled. "Shut up, you bitch."

"Gonna make me, white boy?"

There's a quiet dizzy space. No laughter, just stares. McBride looks on, lips tight.

"I'll make you in my car," Monahan says.

"Whitey's sure lookin' to get killed," Law says, his eye trained across the room.

"Try it, spade." That was Crown.

Law makes a move to rise and so does Crown.

"You make me sick," McBride says.

"Oscar," Jennie lilts. "That's with a *O*, like in 'Oreo.' "

Crown and Law look at McBride.

"Shut up, little girl," he says. And he says it through his teeth.

I don't know if it worked or if some pill she's taken has arrested her, but Jennie doesn't reply. She slouches with a funny little smile.

McBride takes two steps forward. "I pity you," he says. "And you make me sick. So I'm not going to talk to you."

Who, then?

"Instead I'm going to talk to those of you who don't like all this and who wish these people weren't here." His hands are fists at this sides. "All these weeks I've been trying to tell you about a different time, when things were worse. I've been talking about ideals people have worked for." The class is silent. "We haven't made it to those ideals yet, not by a long shot, not when we have these people here. So the question is, what do we do in the meantime?" I see him tremble. "That's always the question, always has been. What can you do if you're someone who hates to see people always beating on each other and being animals?" His hands unlock. "You hang on, that's what you do. You don't listen to these words. You do the best you can. And in the end you win. They lose."

I suddenly realize that McBride rules in this silence, has gained some invisible hilltop. And with equal suddenness I see why he never used his authority as he could have. Attacked as a man, he wanted to face them as a man, not as a teacher.

But how long can this hold? A faint panic creeps in. There's most of the period left to go. After this, how can he cut back to 1781? Carefully I turn to the faces around me. Crown and Law are in their seats, looking bored or irritated. Jennie's expression is still funny. Monahan smirks; so do a few others. But more faces look blank, and still others are intent—a black girl here, a white guy over there. And it comes to me that these particular faces are those of people who couldn't have been enjoying McBride's trial all this time, who couldn't have been laughing much. How could I not have noticed them till now? In back, Nate looks perplexed.

"That said," McBride continues, "I'd like to get back to what we're here for. And this time we'll stay with it." He returns to the map. "Cornwallis moved north into Virginia, and Washington and Lafayette maneuvered to trap him at Yorktown and hold him there till the French fleet could show up. This was the beginning of the end."

Jennie tilts her head back and stares at the ceiling. "You bore me," she says, sighing.

"Then we're even," McBride says without looking at her. "The British tried to break out as soon as Cornwallis realized the mistake . . ."

So he goes on, without interruption. And as he does, I realize that he's all of us—all of us who are trying, in our own ways, to stick it out.

There's this exultation in me, here with my lunch, to which I don't dare open myself fully. Again and again my head replays what happened, until I catch sight of Rhonda. She's eating alone at a table as empty as mine, on the other side. None of the Wilbur contingent, who are in their usual spot some distance away. I stop eating. She looks frail. Recalling my stone face on the stairs, I'm jabbed by an urge to go over to her. Then lunch period ends.

Same procedure in chemistry—me at the door-side desk and Cameron beside Holly. He's on her right now, though, taking advantage of an empty seat on the white side. Eyeing his profile, I think he'll be a hard one to stop hating. Walker is boring, but I don't care.

I really should get reconciled to the way it is with Holly, settle for nice hellos and small talk.

On my way to Spanish I hear tongues flutter some news that reminds me where I am, the way the bang on a door breaks a dream's veneer. A black guy and a white guy got into a shoving match after an English class. It caused quite a stir.

If Page was ransacking the files for fiesta tapes or another film on jolly Mexico, he came up dry, because this time he tries to teach. After some interplay, he settles into a fractured narrative about his experience with the Peace Corps in Peru. This branches into comments on South American history and U.S. imperialism. Fairly interesting. His primary interest is history, he says. A white guy mutters to his friend that he thinks Page is a fag.

Going to the library, I pass Law's bunch and Nate, but they're conversing in a knot and don't see me. I'm coming to the library doors when I hear raised voices from the office across the hall. McBride's is one of them. A black guy and girl I know from math are outside Mr. O'Donnell's door and seem to be listening furtively. Drawn over, I listen too.

"Oscar, I just wonder if that's what's needed," O'Donnell is saying. "We've taken strong measures. God knows we've been handing out suspensions left and right."

"But is *that* the answer?" McBride returns. "Sending them home to Mother?"

"We seem to have some kind of lid on it now."

"I think that's an illusion, Peter. If there's one thing we've seen, it's that anything can happen, anytime." McBride isn't shouting; he's just calmly emphatic.

"Whatever our intentions," O'Donnell says, "maybe we'd be stirring it up worse."

"What would be bad about saying to their faces what

we've said already, only saying it better?" McBride demands. "The worst process, we can't see it with our eyes, and if we let it go on—" He breaks off, pauses. "We just need this assembly. Tomorrow."

After a moment, O'Donnell speaks. "Carol?"

"I think . . ." Mrs. Jessup begins, her voice lower. "I think Oscar is probably right."

A few other kids have drifted up behind us, trying to hear. Then Miss Bradley appears. "What are you doing?" she demands. "Move away from there."

And we do, quickly.

I think about it in the library. Assembly—tomorrow. Maybe. O'Donnell's cold feet, so surprising and contrary to his Irish toughness, may yet prevail. In any case, McBride has finally made his move. A space opens up in me and I fall into it, realizing an exhaustion I've denied and that no sleep could cure. But right away I snap to. It's still too early for feeling that—way too early.

Maybe it will do no good. Maybe, as I sensed, the precious moment came earlier and McBride failed to grab it. It could be too late. Or perhaps it isn't. Or perhaps there never was a real chance. This whole idea of a chance could all along have been an illusion born of ache, like O'Donnell's "lid on it" (jeez!) or the dollhouse utopia Mrs. Rollins sighed over.

But we'll see. I hope we'll see.

When I leave the library at bus time, Yeager and Toohey and the kid who was smoking on the field yesterday are having a chortle by a radiator. Yeager calls out something once I'm past them, and without quite hearing it I extend a middle finger in his direction and keep walking.

I'm nearly the last on the bus, and Rhonda is there looking grim. "Hi," I say as I sit with her.

"Hi," she replies.

When we go past Cedar Drive, I realize Barry isn't on the bus, and he wasn't in Spanish.

I'm working on my lab report an hour after supper when there's a light thump at my door. Then Dad steps in.

"Can I come in for a minute?" he asks.

"Sure." I turn my chair around. It's the first ime he's been in my room since we moved.

With a ragged breath he sits on the bed, facing me. "Well," he says at length. "Your mother told me what happened to you yesterday."

I'd been hoping she wouldn't. "Yeah?"

He nods at the floor, puffing his cheeks as he does when comments come hard; for him they often do. He rubs his chin. "You know, Luke, your mother and I, we always hoped we could steer you and Rhonda around this sort of stuff." Then he flicks the fingers of one hand. "Well, you know. We knew we couldn't screen it *all* out . . .but we just figured we'd give you a good home, good schooling, the basics. Teach you to stand up for yourselves."

"Yeah, Dad. You did."

He nods and smiles. "Yeah. And you're good kids, always good. Smart kids. Mom and I appreciate that."

I shrug. "Well, we got it easier."

"Well." He shakes his head, his smile gone. "Not so much as we'd like." He looks at the floor again, scratches the back of his neck, and grunts. "Can't quite remember what I was gonna say."

We wait.

"Back in Baltimore," he says, "when I was your age, I took my share. The bad names, the spit and such." He taps his knuckles together. "Once . . . some white kids, they caught me coming out of the factory. Worked me over pretty good. But I'll tell ya, somewhere out there today, one of 'em's still missing some teeth."

We smile.

"But yeah," he says. "All that stuff. I met some good palefaces, a few. Even then, back there. A lot of bums too, crackers and such. And my school, that was a hole, I guess."

As he talks, a memory flashes from a year ago. I was in the living room back on Douglas Street, playing a Randy Newman album I'd won on a phone-in trivia question to a radio station. Dad passed through the room, then stopped to ask how I could stand that voice. I protested that the record was okay. Then this song came on called "Baltimore." Dad stopped talking, and I could see him harden as he listened. "Ohhh Baltimore/ Man it's hard/ Just to live." The song has this piano in it that keeps fading out and returning. It's slow, spidering up your back, and makes you see factories, tenements; I guess you'd have to hear it to understand. Dad stood listening till the song was over. Then he puffed his cheeks. "That one's okay," he said, and went to the bathroom.

"So when we settled in Washington," he's saying, "we were both grown up enough to know things we were up against. But we did okay. Your mother had to work, but that was all right. Then, after Fred Jr. . . . well, that was rough. But we wanted children." His eyebrows arch to the wall. "Not as many as your Uncle Earl—"

I laugh, and he laughs a little.

"But we wanted 'em," he goes on. "And you came along. Man, I thought your momma was gonna spoil you. But that never happened. Then we had Rhonda, pretty little thing. I could tell you were both gonna be smart as whips. And life was fine. We had our troubles, all those moves, but mostly it's been fine ever since."

I nod, my hands entwined behind the chair.

He sighs. "So now we're here . . . Sometimes I kind of wonder if it was right . . ."

I shake my head. "I'm glad we're here, Dad."

"Yeah, well . . . It's good you feel that way." He pauses, claps his thighs and gets up. "I guess I really didn't know what I was gonna say." He looks at my desk. "That for science?"

"Yup, chemistry. That's my hardest course."

"Well, I'll let you get back to it." He pats me on the shoulder and leaves.

I turn my chair around but don't pick up the pen.

That was one of the very few times I've heard Dad mention Fred Jr., and it's the most he's ever said about him. A long time ago, Mom told me it was Dad who found the baby dead in his crib. Fred Jr. would have been two years older than I. Sometimes I wonder, as they must, what he would have been like. Zeke Harding, Dad's friend at work, has a son I knew slightly at Randolph, where he's a basketball star. Dad was good at sports. Maybe Fred Jr. would have been too.

I'm thinking this when another knock comes—a sharp one-knuckler.

"Come in."

Rhonda enters—another first—her face unchanged since the bus. She closes the door tightly.

"What can I do for you?" I ask, turning.

She drops onto the bed. "You can tell me why you snubbed me at school. Like I was poison."

"When?"

"You know *when!* On the stairs!"

"That bothered you? Why?"

"It just did."

"So you think I *owe* you?" I yell.

And the next moment the lines appear and she starts to cry. I lean over, put my arms around her, and wait for her to shove me off, but she doesn't. She cries.

"When I went to the hospital," she says hoarsely, "Wilbur was there all broken up, with this tube attached to him. He hardly even recognized me."

"I wondered how it was," I say.

"I couldn't take it," she says, and I feel her body knot up. "Every time I see white . . . I want to just rip it to pieces!"

"I know," I say, holding her tighter. Then I let go and sit beside her. "But you gotta fight that off. That's the game they want."

She wipes her face. "Yeah, sure. So how do I—" She stops, staring past me. "Luke, is that . . . Why is that there?"

I look, and it's the rock on my bureau.

"I thought I threw that away," she says. "You don't

want that thing around." She starts for the bureau, but I hold her arm.

"No, don't," I tell her.

"But why would you want to keep a thing like that?" she demands, eyes wide. "For a conversation piece?"

"I don't know," I say, shaking my head. "I don't know why."

She gives a rough sigh, and I let her arm go.

"What's the story with you and Holly Cliff?" she asks.

"No story. She's scared. I guess I am too."

"Well, that's smart."

"I won't ignore you anymore."

"Thanks," she says tiredly. " 'Night." And she walks out. Going to bed early, I guess.

I go to the bureau and pick the rock up. Pressing it in my hand, I ask myself why I've kept it. No answer. Except maybe that as I stare at it I want to see it eventually crumble of its own accord.

Minutes later I'm outside on the steps, in the cool darkness, with leaves rustling. And those leaves sound like they're trying to tell me something in a tongue I don't quite know. Something about tomorrow.

October 8th

Rhonda and I have taken a seat when Nate comes running down the sidewalk and just makes it on. Breathing hard, he stands by the driver for a moment, then goes past us down the aisle, eyes lowered.

The sky is overcast.

There was something on the cornerstone this morning —in red, the stain says—but the old janitor has gotten it off, making the final scrub as we enter. This time he stays hunched and doesn't look at the kids.

Irwin delivers the roll call rapid-fire—a couple more are missing. Then he announces an all-school assembly for the fourth period, eleven o'clock.

My head is clear. But the numbers on the clock face are suddenly charged with hidden power, as if they'll flash when a hand touches them.

When I get to English, an impulse goes twang in me, loud, like a guitar string, and I take a front seat on the white side. My spine tells me I'm getting looks from both sides, but I don't check, just wonder how so simple a thing can feel so funny. Then Miss Bradley is up there shaking her head over the absences, and my action is complete.

Bradley's mood seems no better than it was yesterday, but there are no scoldings this time. I answer a couple of questions.

Nine o'clock. Going to math, I pass Cameron. He doesn't look at me but I see his shoulders lift. I hope he caught what I was thinking.

Damn Irwin. Damn Irwin and his telegraph chalk, just a bit more staccato than his voice. What business does a guy like this have teaching?

Something's come loose within me, I feel. Raw thoughts whip around in me, but maybe they're just meant to deflect the looks I'm getting, here on the white side. Irwin gave me a double take as class began. On my right a white guy stares from the corner of his eye, but then I see it's quarter to ten, and stop caring.

In back, a voice whispers, "What's it gonna be about, have you heard?" Irwin requests attention.

Ten o'clock—*flash*.

The hum of voices is high through the school as I head for the library. Questions and rumors, rumors and questions—what's it going to be? About Mrs. Hoffmann? The cornerstone? The time of the assembly is unfortunate for me; with no teacher's voice to hold my mind back, it will barrel straight toward what's coming. I doubt I'll get any studying done.

And I don't. Why'd I even bring my books? At a corner table I await the bell—the last bell, as far as I'm concerned. Mrs. Wells stays behind her counter and goes through a catalogue drawer, looking unhappy. Page reads a book.

There's lots of talk. In fact, we may as well be in the halls. Everyone has caught a scent that increases by the minute. Law's table has caught it, and it seems to have fired them with the suspicion that this could be their hour. Law smiles, his men snicker, Jennie is animated, and Nate listens closely, smiling on cue. Happy with your friends, Nate? So there they are, and I imagine that elsewhere in the building, Crown and his boys are sniffing the same thing.

The first two periods clipped by as if the clock had lost its composure, but now it has regained it to mimic a glacier. A minute . . . five . . . ten . . . twenty. Outside, the flag hangs limp. Then it's a quarter to, and I realize I'm inside McBride's head, feeling the hour crawl, knowing so well that what's ahead will be more than just words from a stage. Take a breath. Sometimes I wish I still prayed. Five minutes. Amid the hum, Jennie cackles.

Eleven o'clock—*flash*. And there's the bell. Despite the near-scramble, I'm first to leave.

All over, rooms gush and in a minute the halls are nearly choked. The babbling borders on clamor as kids make for their lockers. I make it to mine by keeping close to the walls, and I've just put my books inside when Holly steps out of the current. Her face has something to say. Now?

"Luke, I didn't want to wait till chemistry to talk to you."

"Go ahead," I say.

"What I said the other day—I didn't want it to hurt like it did. What I mean is . . ." Her fingers play with each other, her face uncertain. "I like you a lot, and it was getting me nervous."

"I like you a lot too," I tell her. "I didn't want us to go strange on each other."

She looks down. Behind her, the hall flows. It's loud. "There's people I've been getting messages from, and I don't mean in words." She looks at me again. "I think the messages were about you."

"Yeah." I nod. "I got ones about you."

"You know, you try to ignore them . . ." Her expression sharpens. "Is that a bruise?"

I'd forgotten about it. "A guy named Yeager did that."

"John Yeager?" Her eyes go wide. "That pig!" She reaches toward my face but her hand stops, inches away.

"Could've been worse," I say.

Just then a fight starts by a drinking fountain and people leap aside. Another black guy and another white guy, beating on each other. Mr. Walker and a black male teacher run up and pry them apart. Hugging her handbag, Holly watches with her back to the locker. I put my hand on her shoulder.

"You wanna go?" I ask.

"Yeah, let's go."

She tags close behind as I wade through the quickly thinning corridors. The auditorium is a separate wing, long and wide and echoey.

On the stage, O'Donnell stands with his arm on the podium. In a fold-out chair to the left of him is a man in a police uniform, and beside him sits McBride. At the right of the podium sits Mrs. Jessup, hands folded in her lap, O'Donnell's chair beside her. The cop gets up and has a word with O'Donnell. McBride looks very small, smaller than the others.

Most of the other teachers occupy the first two rows to the left of the stage. Many students haven't found seats yet, and some stand talking in the aisles, in groups of black and groups of white. The rumble of voices fills the auditorium like a cloud. The light could be better.

The cop takes his seat again, and O'Donnell adjusts the microphone with a crunch. "Could you all get located as quickly as possible?" he asks.

Holly and I find two seats on the end of a row of younger white kids, freshmen or sophomores. I sit on the end and wish we were up further, where at some point I might be glimpsed by McBride. "Who's the cop?" I ask Holly.

"Chief Garfield," she says. "They call him the Fat Cat."

"All right," O'Donnell says, leaning into the mike. "There are plenty of seats. Could you shut the doors back there, please?" The old janitor and a younger one close the doors. "Okay," O'Donnell says, "Let's have it quiet. Quiet please."

The noise falls to a simmer and dies as the principal gets down to business. He clears his throat. "We're here this morning to hear about a problem we're all aware of. The recent assaults and other incidents have brought up something . . . very upsetting. This type of thing has no place here at Bently, and we all have to learn what we can do to stop it. We're fortunate to have with us Chief Daniel Garfield of the Flower Heights Police Department. Afterward we will hear from Mrs. Jessup and Mr. McBride, but right now I hope you'll listen closely to what the chief has to say."

There are sporadic claps as the chief rises and steps up, a few whistles and cries of "Fat Cat!" as he lowers the mike. His badge glints. "During the past month," he says in a resonant bass, "Flower Heights, and this school in particular, have seen a rash of crime that beats anything I've seen in my six years as police chief. I speak mainly of assaults perpetrated by students on students, and assorted mischief such as vandalism and defacement of public property."

Kids look at each other. A few titter. "Wooo!" one voice says low, behind me.

"One very unpleasant aspect of all this," Garfield goes on, "is the race aspect. Now, I'm not taking sides—"

Laughter ripples. Across the aisle, a black guy grins. "No, he ain't takin' sides."

O'Donnell gets up and leans to the mike. "Could we have quiet?"

The noise slides away. Holly gives me a glance.

"Thank you," says the chief, looking disgruntled. "I'm not taking sides here. I don't care about that, whether it's black beating on white, white on black, or whatever. All I know and all we on the force are concerned with is the end result. If a crime, *any* crime, is committed by one or more of you students, we will deal with it quickly and strictly!" He thumps his fist on the podium.

"Wooo!" from behind, two voices this time.

"So just let this be a warning," the chief says, raising his voice. "Any student who hurts another, or who defaces property . . ." And on he goes, thumping the podium, lips thin with conviction.

McBride is looking into his lap. It comes to me that this part of the program is almost certainly O'Donnell's baby, an addition he made after approving the idea. I

158

doubt very much that McBride conjured up the chief.

After twenty or so minutes of dire warning, as it appears that Garfield is winding down, the noise bubbles up again.

"So remember," he says, "it starts with you, and it ends with us. Where you're concerned we'd rather not have to act, but we will if we have to." He pauses, seemingly stuck. "So why don't you get back to studying . . . and try to be friends. Thank you."

He sits to a burst of clapping, whoops, and whistles. "Let's hear it for the Fat Cat!" cries the guy across the aisle.

Mrs. Jessup goes to the podium and adjusts her glasses. The audience settles down for her. Though she's been vice-principal for more than a year, she's kind of an unknown quantity—a Smith grad with careful tones.

"It is sad," she begins, "that we are forced to address this issue. As your vice-principal I've seen the toll this is taking on all of you, though you yourselves may not. I see it in faces, both black and white, even when you smile or say you don't care. The teachers and guidance counselors see it too, every day. But I believe this trouble is coming from a relatively small number of students who are frustrated, mostly with themselves, and who seek targets on the outside . . ."

It's a fair speech, dignified and neatly delivered from note cards. And people are quiet for it, though some wedge deep in their seats and either whisper or seem to doze.

"A change can come, and it has to come," she says, "when you realize what a hurtful word or action from yourself does to you. How each time it makes you meaner, smaller, and less of a person than you could be." She pauses. "Now I'll hand the podium over to Mr. McBride.

Patches of applause open as she sits and McBride stands. Holly and I start to clap, then stop, feeling foolish. From different corners come whoops and whistles. "Heeere's Oscuh!" someone yells from the back; it sounds like Monahan.

Holly puts her fingers to her lips. "Good luck, Oscar," she whispers. Our hands squeeze lightly together.

I press one foot down on the other and stare over the front rows to the stage and the light-brown face, trying to project my spirit—all of it—so he'll feel it and know I'm here. Holding his lapels, he looks out upon the rows stretching back into the dimness. Again I'm seeing through his eyes—bank upon bank of faces. Another whistle. Then he speaks.

"There are some situations we pick ourselves, and there are others that we don't pick and can't get out of. This is the second kind." Reasonable quiet. "So you're sitting here now at a school in Flower Heights, in the United States of America."

"Nooo," comes an acid voice, far on the other side.

Up front, Lattanzio stands and turns. "Shut up!" he booms, and the laughter trickles out. Holly fiddles with her handbag strap.

McBride's hands fall slowly from his lapels to rest on the podium. "If the dice had rolled differently," he continues, "it could have been the Bronx, or South Boston, or Los Angeles, or Russia. But it's not, and you didn't pick it. You also didn't pick what you hear or the things that happen around you. But you're here, and given that, what do you do? We're on a bad ride, getting pulled in a direction that's bad for all of us. Every day the sick words are shouted and the punches are thrown. Think how boring it would be if you weren't so scared . . ."

That's it, McBride. Paint your own kind of message, my kind. The kind that can't be scrubbed away.

"What I'm trying to let you see is that there's an element of choice here; even people in concentration camps have discovered that. But the less say you've had in making where you are, especially if it's bad, the more helpless you feel. That's why people like to make things definite, try to nail them down so all they have to do is look around and they'll know the score and feel safer. Call somebody a name, like 'nigger' or 'whitey,' and that's all they are to you for good. You've color-coded them. Simple."

In the pause, O'Donnell crosses his legs, and so do several people in the audience. The chief looks on, thin-lipped. Mrs. Jessup sits round and dark, a primitive sculpture.

"But whenever people do this, they're fooling themselves, and they're also doing something worse. In trying to be more in control, they lose control. They play right into this game that nobody invented, just let it pull them along." He cups a hand, leaning forward. "What they don't see, and what I'm telling you now, is that you can choose to rebel against it, to stand on your own instead of being a little robot programmed by something sick."

I think of the monster, the black-and-white beast beneath the floorboards in McBride's classroom, how I felt it crouching, laughing to itself. And for this moment it's that thing I hate. Not Crown or Toohey or Monahan or Cameron or Jennie or Law, or even Yeager. I hate the monster.

"That's what I'm asking you to do," McBride says. "Rebel. Some of you already have . . . and I respect you more than I can say."

Thanks.

"Shiiit!" someone says loudly. Lattanzio turns and glowers.

McBride glares in the direction of the voice and doesn't speak. Silence seems to pour in through the shut doors, down from the ceiling and the high windows. A soundless deluge. McBride hunches as he leans further forward. "Yeah," he says. "Easy for you, my man. If you can still think, think about this—maybe you haven't seen certain things before. I mean bigger, badder things. Like a kid lying with a bloody head on the sidewalk, hit by a rock on the first day of classes!" His voice climbs to a shout. "Or whole *crowds* of kids pelted with rocks! Or kids who meant no harm at all getting their faces slammed against lockers! Or grown people, parents, screaming murder at each other outside the school, with their kids watching! Or . . ." He stops. All I'm aware of is his small, still shape, his face drawn tight. Then his shoulders ease and he stands up straight again. His words come out level and clear. "Or just people looking helpless and turning mean because they don't know what's going to happen to them."

The quiet stays, like a mountain on top of us. "But you're not helpless," he says, with a calm now that echoes. "You can rebel. And that begins when you realize how arbitrary everything is. If someone attacks you, decide how to defend yourself. But never forget that but for a slip of chance, that person could have been you, and you could have been him." He steps away, about to sit, but turns again to the mike. "This isn't preaching. I'm right in this with you."

"Sit down, half-breed!" Like a whiplash it comes from the other side, far in back, but I'm not sure McBride hears it in the rush of chatter as he sits.

Out in the halls the lunch bell rings. Holly and I wait in the rumble as the auditorium begins to empty. The younger kids in our row rush wordlessly past our knees. Holly is still fiddling with her handbag strap, and smiles tiredly. "That was good," she says. "He was beautiful." I nod.

On the stage, McBride sits alone while O'Donnell and Jessup speak with the Fat Cat. Garfield shakes hands with all of them and walks off.

Holly and I eventually get up, and as we walk out I have a sensation I'm not used to—calm, deep down. But there's a sour tinge to it. "Sit down, half-breed"— I heard it very distinctly, even if McBride didn't. But I'm resigned, calm and resigned. Miracles are for the Bible, and it's enough to know that he tried, tried his best.

Mobbed as the hall is, we move slowly toward the cafeteria. "You know," I say to Holly, "you don't have to have lunch with me if you don't—"

"I want to, Luke. The hell with it."

"You're a good soldier."

"So are you."

"I think Chuck Cameron hates me, you know that?"

She rolls her eyes. "The hell with him too."

I glance at her, several inches below my shoulder, and a small warm wave goes through me. It's still passing when a figure up ahead jerks away from the cafeteria entrance, elbows flashing. A space clears and it's Toohey. Facing him is Powers, the thickset one from Law's gang. We halt.

"Kiss off!" Toohey shouts.

"Just watch where you going, you white fruit," says Powers. He faces Toohey with half-raised fists, jaw forward.

Some kids squeeze around them to get into the cafeteria and others remain. Holly and I stand to one side in time to let Crown pass, followed by Monahan and two others.

"Lay off, black bastard," Crown spouts.

Powers looks nervous.

Toohey fires up. "Yeah," he says, "you want me to kick your head in?"

"Try and you die, whitey," Powers replies.

Crown takes a step forward, and Power's fists snap all the way up. "Think you're hot shit, don't you, nig?" Crown grins.

I look around for a teacher, but what I see is Law arriving with two of his number.

"Oh no," Holly murmurs.

Law comes up behind Crown and shoves him by the shoulder. Crown whirls.

"Come on," Law says. "Come on."

As they face each other, frozen, I notice Yeager behind Toohey, by the door. By the wall opposite us, Nate looks on. In the eyes of each is an anxious flame.

Then, from the right-hand corridor, Page approaches. Hands spread, he halts before Crown and Law. "Come on, you guys!" he yaps. "Use your heads! This is no good!"

"Shut up, fag!" Crown growls.

Page stares, his mouth hanging. "N-no, come on, you guys!"

"Screw off." Law sneers.

Taking Holly's arm, I squeeze her around behind Page and in the door. "I'll find you," I say.

"Be careful," she blurts.

Returning to my place, I wonder why I feel the need to see what happens. Then I notice Powers looking at me. "Still humpin' that white bitch?" he says.

"You still an asshole?" I say, and suddenly I'm the center of attention.

"Hey, Luke," Law says. "You looking pale, man."

"All right!" Toohey grins. "Nigger fight!"

My face goes tight, my gut like a fist. "Shut up!"

"Fix your window yet?" Toohey says.

Distantly I hear Page gibber. "All right, you . . . you guys shut up before something bad—" My eyes are on Toohey.

"You boys don't listen too well, do you?" My eyes jerk left, and there's McBride standing behind Law, who turns.

"Get outa here, half-breed," Law says.

McBride's look is steady. "Why do you act like such a fool?"

Law goes to shove him, but McBride takes a backward stride. "Just because they're jackasses doesn't mean you have to be one too."

"Tell him, Oscar!" Monahan yelps.

In the next breath Law slips out a blade, *click*. He extends his hand toward McBride, and my stare catches on the thin silver. I shudder.

"I'll cut your ass!" Law says loudly—no cool now.

Page licks his lips and rubs them with an ashen hand. In the crossfire of eyes, McBrides stands solidly, hands ready. My muscles tingle. I've seen this man bear enough; I won't see him get cut. But that knife . . .

"Put it away, George," says McBride. He's angry. "Believe me, you're gonna pay if you—"

Crown lunges at Law's back, but Law spins on a dime. A swipe, a yell, and Crown buckles. Then McBride is on top of Law, struggling. The knife drops and Law throws McBride off. As Law goes to pick it up I take a step, but a tight-shirted hulk drives into him from nowhere—Lattanzio.

"Leggo me!" Law foams.

A second before, the gang members were poised to plunge in. Now they hesitate before the locked mass of muscle. Crown rolls on the floor.

"Keep back!" McBride yells.

Page grabs Law by the legs, gets his jaw kicked, but regains his grip. Flushed and straining, Lattanzio pins Law's arms, and they start moving him down the hall.

"Leggo!" Law hollers. "Leggo me, you white—"

"Hold that nigger!" Toohey yells, jumping, grinning after them. A bolt goes down my arm, and I punch his face. As he stumbles back I see I've split his lip; blood streams down his chin. Next a fist digs into my side and I go down. For a moment I think I'm going to puke, and when I look up, McBride is shoving Yeager away. Toohey holds his mouth and seems dazed. McBride yells. Powers and Monahan are fighting. Then Walker comes running up to separate them. The cafeteria entrance is crammed with onlookers. Rolled up, Crown shivers at their feet.

"Someone run to the office and tell them to call the rescue unit," McBride orders, and the short touchdown kid from gym scoots off.

Then McBride turns to me with a crumpled look. I look away. "I'm sorry," I mutter. He starts to reach down, but I rise. "I'll be okay," I say.

Monahan blurts a curse and Powers goes for him again, Walker straining between them. McBride goes to help. From a short distance down the hall, Nate watches, motionless, like a small kid.

Then I'm walking down the deserted adjoining corridor, leaving the shouts behind. Out an exit, and in a minute I've crossed the grass and am headed down a curving street, away from the yellow-brick building and the beast laughing after me.

I don't know where I'm going; I just keep walking past one house and compact lawn after another. A beagle barks at me from a driveway, an old white lady hangs clothes, and despite my aching side and the blood on my knuckles, the reality of what I've just left is dissolving, its memory already more distant than the block I've traveled. Inexplicably, the deep calm is back, just as before. I keep going.

The sight of these porches brings another kind of resignation. Here is the main fiber of this country I happen to live in. Healthy or sick, this is it. I will never belong to it, not really. Behind these doors and windows, people eat and sleep, laugh and argue. And these people are white. Me, I'm of the fringes. A refugee, finding less to like than I'd wished. Poetic again.

A sleek car drives past with a white man at the wheel.

For the first time since I was small, time is meaningless. As the streets go by, my feet hardly feel the pavement. And I don't know how long or far I've walked when I notice one rundown house, and another further on. I pass a dirt lot with a rusted car, then a corner store with broken bottles around it, and realize I'm out of Flower Heights, entering a section of the North End.

An old black man carries groceries across the street. A group of little black kids run down the sidewalk and into an alley, screeching. Suddenly the city surrounds me once more. Never has it seemed so real.

Up ahead I see tenements—dingy, the color of smoke. The sky is leaden and I feel a chill. My jacket is back at school. I keep walking, watching. Two men talk on a peeling porch. It's garbage-collection day, and bags and battered cans are heaped at the curb. My steps are slower, and then, despite the chill, I stop. I stop in the middle of it all—the tar-papered buildings, the garbage, and the alley screeches. If I kept going, through a piece of the business district and into the city's heart, I'd come to where we used to live. From the top story of one building, between curtains, a woman stares down with her head in her hands. I stare up at her, and for an instant see my own face between those curtains. Down the street, a car honks. "A slip of chance," McBride said. A slip of chance.

I touch my side, and it occurs to me that my father's workplace is maybe a mile from here. So I start walking again, in that general direction.

After I've turned down another, grayer street, I note a police cruiser on the other side, with two white cops in it. I'm directly across from it when one calls out, "Hold it up, there." I stop to look over and he's out of the car, shutting the door. He comes across—a short guy with an eager gait.

"I don't like the way you're walking," he says, halting at the curb.

"The way I'm . . . ?"

"You drunk or something?"

"No, I'm not feeling too well. I've got a pain in my side." I think he plans to add to it.

"Uh-huh." He steps onto the sidewalk. "You got a job?"

"I'm still in school."

"Why aren't you there now?"

"I'm not feeling good today."

"Then how come you're out?"

I look over at the other cop, who gazes calmly from the cruiser while eating a hamburger. "I'm going to meet my father so he can take me—"

"How 'bout putting your hands against that wall and your feet back?" He points.

I look at him, then turn slowly and spread my palms against the chipped brick wall.

"Feet a little further back," he says.

Moving them back, I chuckle.

"Yeah, it's funny," he says, slapping my pockets and hurrying his hands down my legs. "You're a funny person."

His hands feel like a small animal scurrying over me. Then he touches my side and I wince. "I've got a bruise there," I say.

169

"Well, sonny boy," he says, "you'll end up with more than that if you don't stop wandering around like a junkie."

"I take my drugs in private," I say, feeling dizzy.

"Good idea," he says. "You can go."

"Gee, thanks, officer."

"Funny person."

As I move on, a lady with a broom stares from a doorway. Two little girls in dirty shirts watch me pass, one hugging a fire hydrant. I stuff my hands in my pockets. My legs are tired, and my only thought is of getting to Dad.

A fat white garbage man in overalls dumps a can into a truck. A black boy on a bicycle bumps the curb and falls. The big man puts the can down and, with a pudgy grin, goes over and helps the kid up.

Blank-headed through the traffic and storefronts of downtown. Through the sweep of people and window reflections, wondering only whether I can find the place.

I do. A low, ranch-style building with a lot out front and "Eagle Landscaping" on a sign, under the bird symbol. There's our car, parked in welcome.

The secretary, a red-haired lady, looks up in surprise when I enter. She asks can she help me and I ask if Fred Parrish is around. He's out on a job, she says. I ask can I wait for him here and she says certainly and hands me a copy of *American Landscaper*. Thanking her, I sit in a plastic chair.

The clock says three-thirty. I look through the magazine, then put it down and start to doze.

"Are you okay?" the lady asks, her face concerned.

I smile to reassure her. "Just a little worn out."

She types, stopping to munch an apple. The rest is nice for my legs.

In my doze I split Toohey's lip repeatedly, and Yeager punches me repeatedly.

I awake and ask to use the bathroom. When I return, Zeke Harding has just come in.

"Hey!" he says, smiling hugely. His handshake is a squisher, though.I can tell that my name escapes him.

"How you been?" I ask.

"Fine. How's life in the burbs?"

I shrug. "Adjusting."

He laughs. "Good, good. Your daddy'll be along in a little bit. Nice to see you."

He leaves the office and I sit again. Outside the light is low; the clock says five. I nodded off for longer than I thought.

I wait.

Then he comes in, pants dirty to the knees. In the moment before the secretary motions to me and he looks, I take in the sight of him. The stocky warrior, smiling a bit, almost serene. This is his five-o'clock working-day self, which I've never glimpsed.

"Hi, Dad."

"Hello." He stares. "What are you doing here?"

The sky starts to sprinkle as we drive home. My stomach growls; supper will be good. When we get there, Mom and Rhonda are relieved and mystified.

171

October 9th

McBride is not in school.

He's not here. And the person I'm looking at, standing by McBride's desk, is Page. "Mr. McBride couldn't be here today, so you have me," he reveals.

Why isn't he here?

All morning the school's been in a kind of lull that even the absences—ten in homeroom alone—can't explain. The stares I've gotten in the halls remind me that I'm a souvenir from yesterday's drama.

On the bus Rhonda told me how it was after I left— the rescue unit, mayhem in the office, the cops. And Monahan punched McBride. But he was okay, she said. Just shaken up.

"I understand you've been studying the American Revolution," Page is saying. "If you'd like to use this period for review for the next exam, that's fine by me. It's a favorite subject of mine." He reaches for the textbook on the desk. "So, you wanna do that?" Someone in front shrugs. "Okay," he says.

From the low talk of homeroom, I got the state of affairs in detail. Crown wasn't hurt badly and was released last night from the hospital. Powers and Monahan have been suspended. Law is going to be expelled.

Nate didn't show at the bus stop. If he had, I think I might have said something. I don't know what—something conciliatory, maybe. About how he was right, we do have to stick together . . . but in a way that certain things aren't sacrificed. And no, we're not going to let anyone hold us down. Not anyone.

Mrs. Rollins is back. There she was in English, smiling cherubically, clasping the book to her chest as we discussed the Lost Generation. She spoke extra gently, bowing her head slightly at times as if in contrition.

Mrs. Hoffmann is back too, her cheek bruised purple and a cast on one forearm. Watching her circulate slowly during study period, I thought of how she could easily have waited till next week to return, leaving her duties to Page's ever-so-gifted hands for just one more day.

I'm on the white side of the room, as I was in math and English. It doesn't feel as strange now. I'll keep doing it, at least till the symbolism of it gets to be a drag. Leaning back, I look around at the vacant seats—Law, Crown, Monahan, Jennie. No Jennie. The class is still, slouched, without a murmur.

They're gone. The people who jabbed and burned him and enjoyed it, they're not here. Why couldn't McBride be here, standing erect in this room that he has won back, the enemy seats empty before him?

"Any questions about battles or anything?" Page asks. "No? Any about the historical figures involved?"

From the time I got off the bus, I realized something's happened to me. I felt ready, not scared. I met the hate yesterday, and though my side hurts some, I'm here and fine. And I saw a man face it on a much bigger scale and emerge whole. Or so I thought.

On the way to math I practically brushed shoulders with Yeager. Stared right at him as he neared, and he picked up his pace without looking at me. Briefly I wondered whether the chance will come to get back at him —a split lip or a kick in the ribs, at the right moment. But now isn't the time for thoughts like that.

I want to talk to McBride, to ask how he is and maybe explain that bolt that went down my arm the instant before I hit Toohey. No one in authority has spoken to me yet about that little matter, or about my off-the-cuff departure yesterday. It strikes me that, going strictly on principle, I could be suspended too. In any case, gym class with Toohey and Yeager will be interesting from now on. Hell, the whole rest of the year will be "interesting."

But I'm not worried. Though it might have turned out differently, and may still, I'm not really thinking about it. What I see so plainly now is how one person's reaction can stall or accelerate hate's onrush.

In times like this, people are like nothing so much as dogs, strays thrown together in a big kennel. Scared in their ignorance of one another, they bare their teeth. There are those who are more this way than others, and who will probably stay so all their lives. Slaves to the whole kennel scene. Always ready, owing to whatever element in their past or nature, to attack and make a bad scene worse.

For the rest of us there's a choice. We can go with the

fear, as others have, and let it shape us. Let it make us another link in a chain reaction that never ends. Or we can rebel, as McBride said. The first thing, it seems, is to understand the fear behind those glares in the hall. Then maybe you can step outside of it.

To step outside of it — that's what I was blindly attempting all along, without the understanding. Though the knowledge does little to help my attitude toward Yeager and Toohey, I have the feeling that someday soon I'll pity them in their slavery.

Any rebellion's risky, but for the first time I feel ready for hate, without that burning inside. When hate comes, I'll face it as best I can. I may have to fight. Whether McBride and I will prevail — that question doesn't seem big next to the simple thought that this way is better.

But still I wonder — will we prevail?

All this I want to tell McBride. But I think of his flaw — that crack he seemed to transcend yesterday — and recall the sight of him caught in that barbed wire of words and eyes.

"The part of the Revolution that always fascinated me," Page says, "is the way we could have lost at different times, you know? I mean, we might've been British subjects still if we hadn't been lucky. Like just before Saratoga—"

The door opens; McBride steps in. He smiles at Page. There's a Band-Aid on his face.

"Oh, hi," Page says, almost dropping the book.

"Hello," says McBride. "Sorry about the confusion. I had car trouble."

"Well." Page smiles. "Take over."

McBride takes the book and Page gangles out.

I'm sitting up straight in my chair. So are some other kids. McBride appears sharp and relaxed. "We're going to have another test a week from today," he says. "But for now we'll move on . . ."

At the end of class his eyes find me, and he smiles.

Holly and I meet on the way to lunch and she hugs me. Small potatoes, but nothing all year has felt better. The looks we get bounce off us. We get into the cafeteria just before another fistfight starts by the doors. Another white, another black. Two teachers break it up.

In chemistry, Cameron comes in and halts when he sees me sitting with Holly. He looks confused, then goes to the far side of the room. How you feeling over there, Cameron?

After class, Holly waits as Walker demands my lab report, which I give to him, and says he'll expect a slip from the office for yesterday's absence. We snicker on the way out. Columbus Day weekend is coming up — three days. We've parted ways in the hall when Holly turns. "Luke?"

We come back to each other. The side of her mouth turns up. "You wanna come over tomorrow?"

"Sure," I say. "How you think it'll go down?"

"Mom and I talked about you a little. I think she'd like to meet you."

Tucking her address and phone number in my shirt pocket, still a little stunned, I smile to think of the stuff people invite on themselves. Well, maybe we'll make it together through these bad times. Holly has guts. I could get to love her fast.

Hoffmann's lips twist a bit as she finds we've gotten nowhere with the material. That cheek looks sore. Barry comments on it when he comes up alongside me after class, then he speaks of the assembly. He was impressed, apparently. Also his voice is clearer than I've heard before, his plain face firmer.

At my locker I think again of McBride and head for his room. I find the door ajar, but the fluorescents are out and he's not there. From the doorway I gaze down the rows of desks, which seem to quiver with a human essence. That's how it feels — as though in the immolation of the past two weeks we've left part of ourselves behind, to inhabit this room always. And I realize I don't have to speak to McBride anyway.

I sit with Barry in the library and when the bus comes we take the seat behind Rhonda. She has a new painting with her, and after Barry gets off I ask for a look. It's the lone figure of a black girl, separated from darkness by a thin glow.

"That's nice," I say, handing it back.

"Mrs. Sokoloski liked it," she says. "She said, 'Your style's taken an interesting turn.' "

As we amble up the sidewalk toward the house, something occurs to me that's half-hope, half-conviction: that the fissure in me has closed, and I won't be returning to that cold, dark place.

Across the street, that neighbor I saw mowing his lawn two Sundays ago is raking leaves. On a lawn further up, a "For Sale" sign stands.

Rhonda mentions hearing that Wilbur has improved and will be sent home in a week. "I wonder how he'll be," she says.

In the kitchen, we find Mom looking through the want-ad section of the paper, and she smiles up as us. When I ask, she says she's thinking about a part-time job.

Dad will be home in a couple of hours.

Up in my room, I sit at my desk and recall what I'd thought about Wilbur, how his entire self invited attack. But that wasn't the whole truth. Anyone who takes any kind of stand can find himself eligible for the role of human sacrifice. McBride knows.

Over on my bureau top, the rock sits. I'm not sure how long it will remain there.